Tragedy
on the Twenty

Can you imagine raising four children under four
during the depression—without a husband?
Harry Fanson was killed in a tragic accident on Highway 20
when his wife was six months pregnant with their fourth child.

Written and illustrated by Barbara A. Fanson

Published by Sterling Education Centre Inc.
www.SterlingEd.com

Read our blog for information
on designing, marketing, or publishing your own book:

http://fanson.net

Tragedy on the Twenty

This book is dedicated to my mom Lois Fanson
who enjoyed helping to research this historical fiction book
and to my daughter Kristen Van Kampen
whose inspiration and encouragement
gave me the determination to write this book.

But sorry, I am not going to add any mermaids.

Or wand-wielding wizards!

Figure 1: Janetta in front of her house
in Fulton in 1951.

Contents

Acknowledgements

This historical fiction book is loosely based on a real-life tragedy that happened in April 1933 involving my grandparents Harry and Janetta Fanson. Thank you Lois Fanson and Marianne Stephenson who seemed to enjoy the trip down memory lane. To my cousin Don Fanson who suddenly produced photos I had never seen before. Kudos to the Archives Department at the Hamilton Public Library and the Hamilton Spectator for preserving history. And thank you to my proofreader and biggest critic Kristen Van Kampen.
—*Author Barbara A. Fanson*

Figure 2: Harry Fanson, wife Janetta, and son Gordon in 1930.

Sun.	Mon.	Tue.	Wed.	Thur.	Fri.	Sat.
			April 1933			1
2	3	4	5 John & Olive Tweedle married	6	7	8 Stanley Cup
9 Palm Sunday Harry's accident	10	11 Stanley Cup	12 Harry dies in hospital	13 Bonnie & Clyde	14 Good Friday	15 Harry's Funeral
16 Easter Sunday	17	18	19	20	21	22
23	24	25	26	27	28	29 Harry's Inquest
30						

Figure 3: Janetta planned a funeral during the Easter weekend.

Sun.	Mon.	Tue.	Wed.	Thur.	Fri.	Sat.
			July 1933			1
2 Greatest Baseball Game	3	4	5	6 1st Baseball All-Star Game	7	8 Amelia Earhart
9 Robert's 1st Birthday	10	11	12	13	14	15
16	17	18 Baby is born	19 Poloroid film patent	20	21	22
23	24 Bonnie & Clyde	25	26 Joe DiMaggio sets record	27	28	29
30	31					

Figure 4: The new baby was born three months after his father died.

Labor Pains

The Toronto Maple Leafs were in the Stanley Cup Playoffs for the second year in a row. Bank robbers Bonnie and Clyde had another shootout with police. The new German Chancellor Adolph Hitler was making changes in Germany, which had the rest of the world taking notice.

While everyone else was planning for the Easter long weekend, Janetta Fanson was planning her husband's funeral.

Tragedy arrived at 10:30 p.m. like a thief in the night and stole everything: her husband, the father of her children, and their dreams of sharing a lifetime *together*. The life Janetta shared with her husband Harry was smashed at the hands of a reckless driver. The dreams they shared of raising their young family in their own home together—shattered.

Life can change in an instant, like it did on that dark and rainy Sunday evening back in April.

The memories of that tragedy on the King's Highway 20 seeped into Janetta's head like a poison leaving venom that would temporarily paralyze her. Unable to move, she would succumb to the horrible thoughts and fears of living a life without Harry. And once again, she was overcome by a river of tears, which fell like a waterfall down her checks and onto her nightie.

A contraction suddenly snapped Janetta back into present day and she let out a deep, throaty moan. She bent forward and grasped her knees hoping this position would help to relieve the pain of the contraction. As the contraction subsided, she sat back in the slightly used green armchair and took a deep breath. Twenty-five-year old

Janetta pushed the bangs of her dark blonde hair out of her eyes and glanced at the clock. Fifteen minutes apart. It's going to be some time yet.

Janetta shudders every time she thinks back to those tragic events three months ago.

Tonight was the night she had been anticipating, but also fearing. Janetta knew it just wouldn't be the same without Harry, but for tonight, she would have to settle for Malvina, her mother-in-law. For weeks, they had been planning how Janetta would deliver this new baby—without her husband. This was her fourth child so she wasn't inexperienced. But now, she was the only adult in a house with three children under the age of four. How would she deliver her fourth child?

She got up and walked into the kitchen, put some water in the kettle, and put it on the stove to heat up. Then she walked into the living room. And then she walked into the kitchen. And then the living room. Then the kitchen.

The kettle on the stove started to whistle. Janetta took the kettle over to the sink and carefully poured the hot water into her hot water bottle. She walked back into the living room and sunk into the green armchair and slipped the hot water bottle behind her back. The heat felt good on her sore back.

Janetta glanced around the living room at all the second-hand furniture that had been given to her by neighbors and family. She was grateful for everything that the neighbors had done: helping to build her a house, giving her previously used furniture and cutlery and stuff. A few neighbors even offered to babysit when she moved.

When she married Harry in 1928, Janetta moved from her parents' house in Tweedside into the apartment above the Fulton Store with her in-laws and didn't need anything. When she moved into this new wood-frame house with her three sons, she didn't have much furniture except two beds, two dressers, and the plates she had received as a wedding gift.

As she felt a cramp coming on, Janetta bent forward in the chair. She glanced at the clock. Still fifteen minutes. When the contraction subsided, she leaned back in the chair against the hot water bottle and took some deep breaths.

Janetta glanced at a photo sitting on a shelf on the other side of the living room: Harry and Janetta holding their first son Gordon. She remembered being pregnant with Gordon—it was an exciting, but scary time. Harry was hoping for a boy that he could play with; Janetta just wanted a healthy baby.

Harry was thrilled when his first child was born. He couldn't wait to throw a ball with him. "And I'm going to teach him how to skate on the pond," he announced one day.

"And when he gets older, you can teach him how to drive. Maybe he'll be a truck driver like you," Janetta added, with a twinkle in her eye.

For months they talked about saving their money and getting their own house—*together*. They would smile whenever one of them said the word *together* and it soon became *their* word.

Harry and Janetta dreamed of moving out of the apartment above the store that they shared with his parents. He loved his parents, but they wanted to raise a family in their own home.

"Let's build a life—*together*," he said when he proposed five years ago.

Three children later—with a fourth on the way—their dream was finally coming true. Well, sort of. She has her own home and healthy children, but Harry's not here to share it. "I know Harry would have wanted me to buy a house with the insurance money," Janetta thought to herself.

Harry and Janetta had three sons: Gordon Harry was three and a half years old, Orval Stanley was two, and Robert Lewis (Bob) had just turned one. The boys were healthy and well behaved, but Janetta was secretly hoping for a girl this time. How nice it would be to have a little girl to dress-up and brush her hair.

Life can change in a single moment. A tragedy can steal your dreams like a thief in the night. And then you're left with bits and pieces that must be put back together. "I must be the glue that will hold these fragments—*together*," she reminded herself. That word—their word—just didn't have the same meaning anymore. Not without Harry. It takes two to have a *to*-gether ... and now, without him, she was a *one*-gether. She sighed. "Why did he have to be standing outside that night? If he had been inside the store at that moment, he would be okay now. *We* would be okay."

She thought back to that Sunday in April, three months ago ...

"The tea will be ready in a few minutes," the sound of Malvina's voice interrupted Janetta's thoughts.

Malvina and her husband, Edward Fanson owned the Fulton General Store on the King's Highway 20 between Hamilton and Niagara Falls. They bought the store in 1924 when their son Harry was eighteen and their daughter Edna was fourteen. For the past nine years, they lived in the apartment upstairs above the store. Their son, Harry, moved his bride, Janetta, in when they got married in 1928. A year later Gord arrived followed by Orv and Robert (Bob). With four adults, three children, and another baby on the way, the three-bedroom apartment was getting crowded.

As another cramp came on, Janetta—or Nettie as most people called her—mooed like a cow while her mother-in-law Malvina applied pressure to her lower back. The cramps were five minutes apart now, so she knew a new baby was imminent.

Janetta sat back in the armchair with the hot water bottle. "If it's a girl, I'm going to name her Harriet," she announced. "If it's a boy, I'm going to name him Harry, after the father he'll never..." her voice trailed off as a wave of tears fell down her cheeks and onto her nightie.

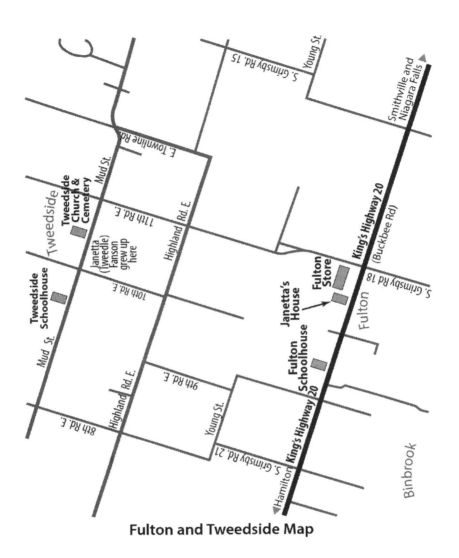

Fulton and Tweedside Map

Life Above the Store

Janetta shook her head in disbelief ... her life was going so well, up until that Sunday in April, three months ago ...

Janetta Tweedle, or Nettie, as friends called her, grew up in Tweedside, Ontario. She was the seventh child in a family of eight children: four boys and four girls.

Janetta walked to the one-room schoolhouse in Tweedside, just like her brothers, sisters, and cousins. Enrollment at the Saltfleet School 8 rose in the 1920s to 50 pupils in that one room. The new red brick schoolhouse that Janetta attended was built in 1908, the year Janetta was born! The new school was built on the foundation of the original stone school that was built in 1865.

Although she grew up on a farm, her father took advantage of the newest inventions to make country living a little easier. By 1909, Janetta's family had a telephone installed and they got hydro by 1926. By this time, there were more telephones in Saltfleet than in Stoney Creek.

By 1917, her father bought his first automobile but only drove it in the summer and spring months. In the winter, he took the wheels off the car and stored them in the house until the roads were passable in the spring.

Janetta lived with her family near the Tweedside Wesleyan Methodist Church, which her uncles helped build. She'd heard the stories of how her Grandfather John Tweedle and her uncles hauled all the bricks up the mountain by horse and wagon from the old Methodist Church in Bartonville to this new location in Tweedside.

When she was eighteen years old, her brother Anson introduced her to his friend Harry Fanson of Fulton. Harry had dark hair, a slim build, and a playful nature. He was quick with the jokes and fun to be around. Harry began courting Janetta and they married on November 29, 1928, when she was twenty years old. She moved in to the apartment above the Fulton Store with him and his parents Edward and Malvina Fanson,

Eleven months later, they welcomed a little boy on October 20, 1929, and named him Gordon Harry. Nine days later, the stock market crashed and the Great Depression started.

A second son Orval Stanley Fanson was born on February 6, 1931, and Robert Lewis arrived on July 9, 1932. When the accident happened in April of 1933, Robert—or Bob, as he was called—was nine months old and they were expecting their fourth child in July. They all lived above the store with his parents Edward and Malvina Fanson.

Some people believe 1933 was the worst year of the depression because thirty percent of men couldn't find work. Harry Fanson was one of the lucky ones. He was ambitious and hard working. He wanted to make enough money so him and Janetta could buy their own house— *together*.

During the day, Harry was driving a dump truck and hauling stones; he helped change several old roads into the King's Highway 20. The old Buckbee Road from Fulton and Smithville became part of the King's Highway 20 in 1930. In 1932, they were changing the route. Instead of taking Rymal Road in Hamilton and turning north on Upper Gage, east on Concession, and then joining up with Highway 6 (Upper James Street) and going down the mountain into downtown Hamilton, the highway was being re-routed to go north through the Stoney Creek Cut, down the mountain and joining Highway 8 or King Street.

During the 1920s, industry in Hamilton was booming and many families could afford to buy an automobile, in any color, as long as it was black. Janetta's brother bought his first car in 1926. So, Edward installed a gasoline pump in front of the Fulton Store. But, during the 1930s, the Fulton Store was not as busy as it had been.

Those who had a job were afraid to spend money; no one knew when the depression would end. People were not buying as much gasoline at the Fulton Store or buying as much food. They grew food in their own gardens, canned whatever fruit they could pick, and just didn't spend as much money as in the 1920s.

Janetta loved Sundays; it was her favorite day of the week; it was the only day that Harry could sleep in, because the store didn't open as early. And that's the morning the boys looked forward to. Sometimes, they snuck into their parents' bedroom, quietly climbed up on the bed, and jumped on Harry.

"Oh, no," he'd say, "there's a bear on our bed!" and then he wrestled with them.

After breakfast, they all went to Fulton Stone United Church together. If it's a nice day, they walked the mile to church, but on that April morning, there was a chance of rain so all seven of them squeezed into Grandpa Ed's car. In those days, you didn't need a seatbelt and children often sat on their parent's knee. It was a special Sunday—it was Palm Sunday. It was the beginning of Holy Week.

After church, Grandpa Ed unlocked the door and opened the store. The rest of the family went upstairs and ate a bowl of homemade soup and fresh bread for lunch, but not Grandpa Ed. Malvina took a bowl of soup downstairs to Ed to eat in the store. When they finished eating, Harry didn't go downstairs to the store right away. It usually wasn't that busy on Sundays during the lunch period.

"I hear something," Harry said right after lunch, "where is it coming from?" He put a pot upside down on his head and put bowls upside-down on Gord's and Orv's head. He took a wooden spoon, a ladle, and an egg turner from the kitchen drawer and gave them each a weapon.

"Ssh," he whispered as he motioned for the boys to get down on their knees and follow him. Orv and Gord got down on their knees and crawled quietly through the kitchen and peeked through the door into the living room.

"Gord, you go that way around the chair," Harry instructed him to go to the left side of the chair in the corner, "and Orv, you go to the right. I'll attack from the top." They crawled quietly around the chair and then all attacked at the same time!

"A bear!" Gord shouted as he held up a homemade stuffed bear. He smiled as he looked at the surprise. He knew Janetta made the bear and sewed on the button eyes. "I love it," he said, as Orv grabbed it away and put it in the back of the toy dump truck. Soon, the bear was traveling around the living room in the back of a dump truck.

Gord looked at Janetta, who was looking at Harry with "those gushy eyes". They may not have a lot of money and they may be living in a depressed economy, but Janetta was good at sewing things and Harry was good at making up games to play. They made a great team—*together*.

Then, Harry said it was time to go help Grandpa in the store and Janetta announced that it was naptime. As Harry went downstairs to the store, Janetta picked up nine-month-old Bob, who had been sitting on the floor and proceeded to her bedroom. She checked his diaper and then carried him into the bedroom that Orv and Gord shared. The old bedsprings of the hand-me-down bed creaked as Janetta sat on the edge of the double bed with Bob on her lap. Gord pushed two-year-old Orv up onto the bed on one side of Janetta, and then clambered up onto the bed and nestled on the other side of Janetta. She told them the story of the Three Little Pigs.

After the story, Orv laid down in the double bed next to the wall and Gord crawled under the blankets next to him. He lay there for about twenty minutes, but he wasn't sleepy, so he crawled out of bed. Gord wasn't napping much any more; after all, he was three-and-a-half. He tiptoed quietly through the hallway into the living room where Malvina was sitting in the corner chair, sewing a button on a shirt. He didn't see his mom Janetta so he assumed she was napping. Since Bob was born nine months ago—and with the new baby on the way—she usually had a nap when the boys did.

"May I go downstairs to the store?" Gord whispered to Grandma. She nodded yes, and he walked quietly down the stairs and into the store.

A Bennett Buggy
Visits the Store

Gord walked into the quiet store and saw his Grandpa Ed standing at the counter reading yesterday's newspaper. He looked around but there were no customers in the store. He looked out the window of the store and could see his dad Harry outside by his dump truck.

"May I go outside to watch Daddy?" Gord asked his Grandpa Ed. He looked up from his newspaper and looked out the window.

"Well, there's no customers right now. Let's go ask him," Ed replied. Grandpa Ed took Gord's hand and walked out of the store and across the gravel to where the dump truck was parked beside the store.

"Hi Daddy," Gord said.

"Hi Squirt," Harry replied and then turned to Grandpa Ed "I can watch him."

Gord smiled his approval. He loves the time he gets to spend with Daddy alone, without Orv or Bob. Harry lifted him up so he could stand on the front bumper of the dump truck and peer into the engine. There were tubes and wires running throughout. And it was dirty and greasy. Harry pulled out the dipstick and showed him the oil dripping off it. "We need to check the oil and make sure there's enough oil because it makes the parts run smoothly," he explained. He put the dipstick back into the oil reservoir. Then he reached up and released the latch to close the hood over the engine. He took Gord off the bumper and put him down on the ground.

"Can I drive your truck?" Gord asked.

"Yep," Harry replied. He went around to the driver's side and opened the truck door. He bent down, picked Gord up, and put me up into the big truck. Gord stood on the seat and turned the steering wheel to the left and then the right. When he stood on the seat, he could also see out the windows. He was so high up he could see really far. He was taller than his Dad!

"Vroom, vroom!" Gord said as he turned the steering wheel in Harry's big dump truck.

"When I grow up, I'm going to drive a big truck like you Daddy," Gord proudly announced. Harry smiled.

One day Harry let Gord go to work with him. Gord sat in the passenger seat beside Harry; it was a really bumpy ride. In 1933, no one wore a seat belt. In fact, seat belts didn't become mandatory until 1976. Gord had to stay in the truck but he could look out the back window as a front-end loader scooped up a pile of stones and dumped it into the back of his dad's truck.

Then they drove to a road construction site on the newly named King's Highway 20. Harry had to back up the truck and then the scoop on the back of the truck went up and Gord couldn't see anything from the back window. But, he could hear it. He heard the stones sliding down and out of the truck as the truck slowly moved forward. He helped stone the new highway! Although the official name in 1930 was the King's Highway 20, most people just call it Highway 20. It won't be called Buckbee Road anymore.

Highway 20 runs between Hamilton and Niagara Falls. Janetta and her family live in Fulton, 16½ miles (27 kilometers) from Hamilton. Harry said the road construction was a government project to provide work for people during the depression. They are going to put down stone all along the highway.

Just then, an automobile pulled by two horses turned off the highway and pulled up to the gas pump. "It's a Bennett

Buggy," Harry said as he helped Gord out of the truck. The term Bennett Buggy or Oatsmobile had become popular this year since some farmers couldn't afford gas for their automobile. During the "glorious 1920s," as Grandpa Ed calls it, everyone was buying automobiles, so Ed had a gas pump installed in front of the store. But since the depression started, some people can't afford to buy gas to run their automobile or to pay for repairs. Horses have become popular again, even if it's just to pull their automobile like a carriage. Harry says the seats in an automobile are way more comfortable than a wagon or carriage.

"You stay here Gord and play in the dirt while I go see this customer," Harry said as he walked Gord over to small dirt pile beside the store. Gord had a wooden truck to play in the dirt, just like his Dad.

As Gord used a spoon to dig a road through the mountain of dirt, he could hear Harry talking to the man in the Bennett Buggy. He thinks the stranger lives near here. The stranger wants to drive to Trenton to an unemployment relief camp but he doesn't have any money for gas. Would Harry give him credit and he'll pay him back? Harry probably feels sorry for the man, but he struggled for the right words.

"I'd like to help, but you're going out of town and that's high risk."

"Can I trade you a pair of shoes?" asked the stranger. "I paid $2.50 for these new shoes a month ago. They look like they'll fit you. How about you give me $2 of gas in exchange for the shoes." Let's call the stranger Bennett.

Harry took the shiny black shoes from Bennett and tried them on. They did fit. And he did need some new shoes to wear to church. "Ok," Harry said, "$2 worth of gas."

"Great," smiled Bennett, and he reached his hand out to shake Harry's hand. "Thank you." Harry put gasoline into the Bennett Buggy and then he took his new shoes into the store.

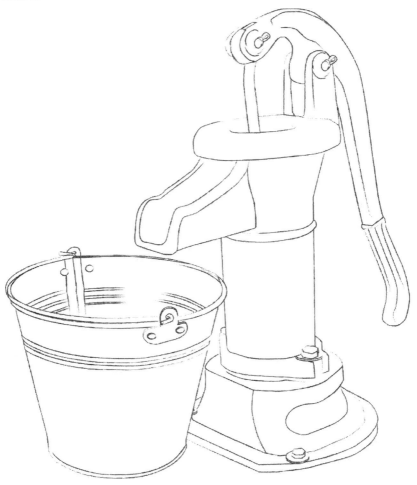

Tragedy on the Twenty

Sunday evening at the store

At dinnertime, Malvina carried two plates of dinner down the stairs into the store while Gord carried a small plate with two slices of homemade bread. "That smells good," said Ed, looking up from Saturday's newspaper. Harry came in from outside and went to the water pump. After a few pumps of the handle, water was pouring into the pail beneath the spout. Harry took the ladle and dipped it into the pail. He scooped some water into the wash pan and both men washed their hands. Soon, they were eating dinner.

"Come on Gord, let's go upstairs and eat our dinner," Malvina said as she and Gord went back up the stairs. On Sundays, they usually have leftovers from Saturday night. Sometimes, Ed trades cow or pig meat for gasoline or groceries. Usually, they have meat on Saturday night, and then heat up the leftovers on Sunday, so they don't have to cook on the Sabbath day.

After dinner, Gord and Orv took a blanket and went downstairs to the store and played with the boxes. They draped the blanket over the four boxes and made a tent—a very small tent that you could only enter if you crawled on your hands and knees.

Before long, Janetta was telling them it was time for bed.

"Just one more minute," Gord pleaded.

"No," Janetta said, "It's time for bed."

"Dada," Orv said.

"Daddy, can you tell us a story?" Gord asked. Harry looked at Grandpa Ed, who nodded approval. "Yay!" Orv and Gord yelled as they ran towards the stairs. They quickly put on their jammies and got into their bed, ready for story time.

"Tell us the story about the snapping turtles," Gord urged Harry, when he came upstairs into their bedroom. Harry sat down on the edge of the old, creaky double bed that Gord and Orv shared, and rested Bob on his knee.

"Once upon a time, when Aunt Edna was eight and I was about ten years old, we walked down a country road to a stream," Harry started the story, "As I stood on the side of the creek, I could see a baby turtle walking on the shore. My Dad taught me to handle a turtle by the back end away from its head, just in case it's a snapping turtle." Harry put his hands together as if there was a hinge at his wrists. He opened and closed his hands like a snapping turtle would open his mouth.

"I barely picked him up when he tried to snap at me! It was a baby snapping turtle.

'Oh, it's so cute. Can we take it home?' Edna asked. We looked around for something to carry it home. We couldn't find anything, so Edna ran all the way back home to get a pail or can, while I stayed and kept an eye on the baby snapping turtle.

She ran back several minutes later with both—a pail and a can. 'Daddy said we should bring back some creek water in the pail for the turtle.' So, we put the baby turtle in the can and scooped up some clear creek water with the pail. Then we carried the turtle and the water back to the house.

Our Mom had a large wash pan that she wasn't using so we put the turtle in it. Mommy added a little dirt on one side of the pan so the turtle could have some 'land'. Then we added a rock and a branch so he could walk on them. We poured some of the creek water into the other side of the pan so he could swim. Mom would not let us bring the turtle into the house, so we had to keep him in the shed.

But then one night, it turned very cold and Daddy said he might freeze outside, so we got to bring him in the house for just one night.

The next morning, Edna woke up first and she saw that there was no turtle in the dishpan. 'Where'd you put him, Harry?' she asked me.

'I don't have him,' I answered and hurried over to the dishpan in the living room. He was gone. We looked everywhere, but we could not find the turtle. I guess he was starting to get too big for the container and crawled out. Mom was hoping he would turn up eventually.

And he did. Mom was cleaning the house on Saturday morning and lifted up the mat in the living room to find a squished turtle under it. He must have crawled under the mat and someone accidentally stepped on him."

"Let's go to the creek tomorrow!" Gord said beaming, "It rained today so there will be lots of water in the creek!" Orv nodded in agreement.

"We'll see," Harry said as he bent over and kissed the boys good night.

Janetta, who had been listening to the story from the doorway, came over and pulled the blanket over Gord and Orv. "Soon, we're going to have move Bob into this bed with you two so the new baby can sleep in his crib," she said as she kissed Orv good night. And then she kissed Gord good night.

"Good night, Mom. Good night, Dad," Gord said.

"Good night, both of you." Harry said as he turned and headed towards the stairs to the store. The boys didn't know that story would be the last story Harry would ever tell them. Or, that they would never say good night to him ever again. It didn't take long for them to drift off to sleep.

Tragedy on the Twenty

At about 10:30 p.m. on Palm Sunday night, both Grandpa Ed and Harry were outside, in front of the Fulton Store. The light rain had subsided. Grandpa Ed was pumping gasoline into customer Bill's car, in front of the store. Harry was talking to Charlie who arrived on a motorcycle and needed some gas. Charlie was sitting on his motorcycle—though it wasn't running—about a foot from the highway. Harry was standing two feet away from him.

When the Fulton Store got hydro in 1926, they installed a light outside on the wall of the store and another on a pole to the side of the gravel parking lot. But, at 10:30 on that spring night, it was still dark.

"Did you hear the hockey game on the radio last night?" Charlie asked.

"Bits and pieces," replied Harry, "between customers. I know that New York beat Toronto 3-1."

"Now, New York leads the series 2 games to 0," Charlie said, somewhat disappointed.

"I know," Harry added, "now Toronto has to win on Tuesday, or New York wins the Stanley Cup 3 games out of 5." (In 1933, there were only five games in a playoff series, but today, it is best out of seven games.)

"Hey, maybe we'll win on Tuesday and Thursday and tie up the series and force a game 5," suggested Charlie, "can you imagine Toronto winning two Stanley Cups in a row!"

"That would be nice," smiled Harry, remembering how the Toronto Maple Leafs won the Stanley Cup last year.

Suddenly, a motorcar went out of control and barreled off the paved highway through the parking lot way too fast!

It missed the motorcycle, but hit Harry and sent him flying up onto the left fender of the car and then landed with a thump on the ground. The out-of-control car swerved and narrowly missed Ed who was pumping gas into customer Bill's car. It sideswiped Bill's car, which was sitting at the gas pump. The out-of-control car swerved to a stop in a cloud of dust and gravel.

And then silence. The loudest silence you ever heard. It happened so quickly, but in slow motion.

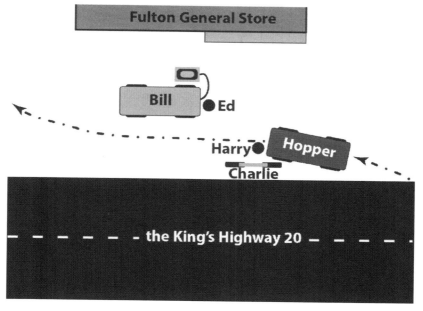

Janetta was suddenly awakened from her sleep by a loud noise outside the store. She looked out the window straining to make out something in the darkness of night. She couldn't see anything in the cloud of dust below the second-story window.

As the dust dissipated, she saw a figure lying on the ground near a motorcycle. Did the motorcycle hit someone? Janetta got out of bed and went into the hallway, just as Malvina was coming out of her bedroom. They both hurried down the stairs to see what happened.

As Janetta and Malvina ran down the stairs and out of the store, Grandpa Ed was hurrying into the store. "I need to phone Dr. Leeds. Harry is hurt. And the police," he said quickly as he ran into the store.

Janetta and Malvina ran to the other two men who were squatting and looking at Harry lying on the ground, near the motorcycle.

Three-and-a-half year old Gord had also been awakened by the crash and heard the sound of feet running down the stairs. He looked out the window and saw several people gathered together in the gravel parking lot below.

"Daddy," he yelled as he jumped out of the bed and ran through the hall. He ran down the stairs and through the store. As he ran out the door of the store towards Harry, he was suddenly grabbed from behind.

"Let me go! Let me go!" Gord yelled while trying to wriggle out of someone's grip. A hand went over his mouth so he couldn't yell. Whoever had grabbed him from behind carried him back into the store.

"Gord," Grandpa Ed said as he put Gord down, "there's been a bad accident."

That's all he heard as thoughts raced through his head. Bad accident? What happened? Grandpa Ed must have said don't go outside, though Gord didn't really hear him. Then, he heard Grandpa Ed telephoning Dr. Leeds to come right away. He was in Smithville and should be here in twenty minutes. Grandpa Ed also telephoned the Ontario Provincial Police who had a detachment in Grimsby.

Grandma Malvina ran through the store shouting "towels" as she vanished up the stairs. She ran back down—two steps at a time! She only stopped long enough to grab the pail of water that sat under the water pump and ran outside.

Gord watched from the window as Grandma Malvina knelt down beside Harry and put a wet cloth on Harry's head. She used another cloth to wipe blood away from Harry's head. Then, they put a folded towel under Harry's head. Grandpa Ed went back out to see if there was something else he could do.

The stranger—Hopper— who caused the accident had been pacing nervously around the parking lot, staying out of the way. Then, he turned and walked into the store. He looked around and spotted onions in the vegetable section of the small, general store. He walked over, picked up an onion and tore the dark, outer skin off. He dropped the outer skin into a nearby garbage and bit into the onion.

"Yuck," Gord thought to himself, imagining how a raw onion would taste. The stranger walked out of the store eating the raw onion, as if it was an apple. He didn't even see Gord standing by the window.

Finally, he wandered near Malvina and looked over her shoulder as she was helping Harry. The scent of an onion tickled Malvina's nose. She looked up "You're eating an onion? My son is hurt and you're eating an onion??!"

"Have you been drinking?" Grandpa Ed asked as he stood up. "Well, have you?" he demanded to know. The stranger shrugged his shoulders.

"Why you..." and Grandpa Ed punched Hopper in the face! The stranger put his hand to his face. The stinging punch on his cold face was painful. Charlie, the motorcycle driver, stepped closer and put himself between the two men.

"I know you're angry," Charlie said to Grandpa Ed, "but your son needs you now."

Ed exhaled loudly, obviously upset. That seemed to settle him down a bit, but he was angry. "He drove a car into my son and he eats an onion?" He turned to Malvina, "And make sure you tell the police that I think this good-for-nothing bum has been drinking." The stranger turned and walked to the other side of the gravel parking lot, his face still stinging from the punch.

Gord watched as headlights from a motorcar turned off the paved highway and into the driveway. The car stopped a few feet in front of Harry, who was still lying on the gravel driveway. A man stepped out of the car carrying a black doctor's bag. Gord recognized Dr. Leeds who knelt down beside Harry. After a quick examination, Dr. Leeds gave him a shot of painkiller or something.

Grandpa Ed picked up a barn lantern and ran quickly around the back of the store. He returned with two of the wooden stakes that he used in the garden in the summer. Gord watched as they put a piece of wood on each side of Harry's leg and tied a rope around his leg to create a splint. Charlie and Grandpa Ed lifted Harry, carried him to the car, and carefully laid him on the back seat of Dr. Leeds' car.

"I'll come to the hospital after the police get here," Grandpa Ed yelled to Dr. Leeds. Janetta got into the front seat with Dr. Leeds and they drove onto Highway 20 and headed west towards Hamilton.

That's when another set of headlights turned into the parking lot in front of our store. As the car door opened, Gord recognized the word POLICE on the side of the car door. Gord watched as Grandpa Ed walked towards the police officer just as Hopper—the driver of the out-of-control car—approached from the other side.

"Let me tell my version first and then I'll hurry to the hospital to see Harry," Grandpa Ed said to Hopper.

Grandpa Ed turned to the police officer and said, "He was eating an onion. That usually implies that he wants to hide some odor on his breath." Grandpa Ed continued with his explanation. Grandpa Ed pointed to Charlie who came on a motorcycle and Bill who was standing by his car at the time of the accident. The police officer took notes as

Grandpa Ed talked. Then, Grandpa Ed said good-bye to Malvina and disappeared down the highway in his own car.

The police officer spoke to the other two witnesses. Charlie, who came on a motorcycle, then Bill, who was standing by his car at the gasoline pump. The police officer was holding a barn lamp near customer Bill's car so he could see the damage on the left side caused by the Hopper's out-of-control car.

The police officer asked Hopper, the maniac driver, for his version of the story. The officer took notes while Hopper talked.

Eventually, they all left and Malvina headed into the store. As she turned to lock up the store, she shrieked, "Oh, it's you! You startled me!"

And then she quickly added, "It's awfully late for a little boy to be out of bed. Let's go upstairs to bed." She carried the lantern and followed Gord upstairs.

Hospital visits
and busy schedules

When Gord awoke on Monday morning, he could hear voices in the kitchen.

"We need to get in touch with Edna." Janetta said, "She should know Harry's in the hospital." Edna is Harry's sister who lives in Binbrook with her husband Jack Leggett and her two children.

"I'll go downstairs to see what Grandpa Ed wants to do," Grandma added. "He's working in the store this morning and right after lunch, he's planning to drive to St. Joseph's Hospital in Hamilton to see Harry."

"I'd really like to go with him," Janetta said, "Malvina, do you think I could get Mrs. Sheldrake to babysit the boys?"

"Maybe ... they will be napping." Malvina replied, "Maybe Nettie, you should walk over and ask her after you get all the boys dressed. I'll stay at the store while you and Grandpa Ed go to the hospital, but I really would like to go and see Harry, too."

"May I go see Daddy, too?" Gord asked.

"Oh, hi Gord," Malvina said, when she realized he had entered the room.

"I don't know," Janetta answered, as she walked closer to Gord. She looked at Malvina and then at me. "He's hurt real bad and he's sleeping. But, he is in the hospital surrounded by doctors and nurses," she tried to reassure Gord.

Just then they heard Bob, the baby crying and Janetta went to her bedroom, where Bob's crib was.

YOUTH WAS HIT BY MOTOR CAR

Harry Fanson, Grimsby, Injured Last Evening

From Our Own Correspondent

Grimsby, April 10—Harry Fanson, 20-year-old son of Edward Fanson, who operates the Fulton general store on No. 20 highway, sustained a fractured left leg, head lacerations and possible internal injuries about 10:30 last night when hit by a motor car in charge of Frank Hopper, 1044 King street east, Hamilton. This injured lad was attended by Dr. Leeds of Smithville, and later removed to St. Joseph's hospital at Hamilton. According to the information given the Spectator reporter at the scene, a car in charge of Bill Bugle, 3234 Yonge street, Toronto, was in front of the Fulton store getting gasoline and a short distance behind it, but also on the driveway off the pavement was a motorcycle in charge of Charlie Spencer, R.R. No. 2, St. Ann's. Young Fanson stood in the driveway talking to Spencer when a west bound car in charge of the Hamilton driver came along and it is alleged suddenly swerved off the pavement to the right of the parked motorcycle, struck Fanson, throwing him over the left fender, and then continued around the driveway narrowly missing Mr. Fanson, sen., and smashing into the Bugle car which was considerably damaged on the left side of the pavement, and then back to the north side where it stopped. Mr. Hopper, the driver, claimed that an eastbound car was approaching him on the wrong side of the road and that he swerved to avoid a head-on collision. The highway was slippery at the time and a light rain was falling.

Provincial Constable W. A. Smith of Grimsby, was called to the scene and made an investigation.

The Hamilton Spectator
Monday, April 10, 1933

In the corner of the kitchen, Gord saw the box Harry brought upstairs yesterday so they could play in it. Gord got on his knees in the box with his hands outside the box. His hands were on the floor pulling him across the floor. Today it is a boat and he is sailing across the sea (the kitchen floor).

His brother Orv woke up soon after and Janetta changed his diaper and dressed him. She walked into the kitchen carrying Bob with Orv following behind.

"Is it okay if I go downstairs to the store to use the telephone? Or do you want some help with the boys?" Grandma Malvina asked Janetta.

"I think I'm okay. You go ahead," Janetta replied.

"Gord," Janetta asked as she turned to him, "Can you and Orv play with the box while I make oatmeal for everyone?" She placed Bob the baby on his tummy on the floor. He crept toward the box. Bob is nine months old so he tries to creep, but he's not walking yet.

Gord got out of the box and helped Orv get in. "Pretend the box is a boat and you're sailing across the sea," he said as he pushed the box across the floor with Orv inside.

After Janetta made the oatmeal, she fed Bob while Orv and Gord struggled to feed themselves. Gord, the older one is much neater than Orv—half of his oatmeal is on his face! Janetta is much quieter this morning than usual. She must have a lot of things on her mind—like Harry. She wants to go see him in the hospital, but she doesn't drive and she has 3 young children. Neither Janetta nor Malvina know how to drive an automobile. Grandpa Ed and Malvina have a store … they can't just leave the store to go see their son in the hospital. One of them has to stay and work in the store. "You don't make any money if you close the store," Grandpa Ed would say.

When the boys finished eating their porridge, Janetta wiped their face and hands with a cloth and brushed their teeth with water and baking soda.

"We're all going for a walk to Mrs. Sheldrake's house this morning" Janetta announced, "I want to see if she can babysit this afternoon."

After the boys were dressed, Janetta put a light jacket on them, before putting on her own jacket. Though she did up their jackets, she didn't do up her own jacket. In fact, her jacket was starting to look a little tight around the waist. Janetta is hoping for a healthy baby girl or boy in the summer.

Janetta picked up Bob and Orv and carried them down the stairs to the store. Gord followed behind. Janetta went behind the counter and through the door into the storage room. She set Orv down while she pulled a baby stroller out of the room with one hand while still managing to hold Bob with the other. Then Gord and Orv followed her through the store and out the front door. Once outside, Janetta opened up the folded stroller and placed Bob in the seat. She lifted the footrest, lifted Gord, and placed him on the footrest at the front of the stroller. Orv stood on the rear axle at the back of the stroller.

"Hold on tight," Janetta advised us, as she pushed the stroller through the stone parking lot towards the highway. She pushed the boys in the stroller along the stone shoulder of the highway.

Spring arrived early and the April weather was warm. Now that the snow has melted, more people are outside, including Mrs. Sheldrake. She was happy to see the visitors and commented how big the boys have gotten over the winter.

"There was an accident in front of the store last night," Janetta said, "Harry was hit by an automobile. He's in St. Joseph's Hospital." Mrs. Sheldrake was shocked.

Mrs. Sheldrake said she'd be happy to look after the boys, and if we needed anything else, please just let her know. They made arrangements for her to walk over to the store at noon. Janetta would feed the boys early and put them down for a nap. Janetta assured her that they would be back before dinner. If she needed anything, Grandma would be working in the store downstairs.

"I want to see Daddy," Gord piped up.

"We'll see," Janetta said, as she turned to Mrs. Sheldrake, "Thank you. See you at noon." Janetta turned the stroller around and pushed it back home.

"I'll be good. Please, can I go see Daddy?" Gord begged, but Janetta was deep in thought as she pushed the stroller through the stone on the side of the highway.

Back at the store, Grandpa Ed was pumping gas for a customer. "Hi Grandpa," Gord yelled.

"Hi, Gord," he yelled back.

Janetta took the boys out of the stroller, through the store, and back up stairs. Gord and Orv raced to the box on the kitchen floor. Gord got in first because he can step over the side of the box to get in. Orv can't. He went in headfirst. "Ouch," Gord said as Orv crawled in the box on top of him. And there they were ... both of them ... just sitting in the box.

"Push," Orv said.

"No, it's your turn," I replied, "I pushed you this morning."

"I have an idea," Janetta said as she went into her bedroom. She returned with a blanket and draped it over the table and two of the chairs. "Now you have a house or a tent." Gord and Orv both got out of the box and went into the tent. Janetta tipped the box over on its side and put it beside the tent. "You can use the box as a room or something."

After lunch, Janetta put Bob in the crib in her bedroom and Gord and Orv in the double bed in their room. Janetta, Harry, and Bob the baby share a bedroom. Gord and Orv share a bedroom. And Grandpa Ed and Grandma Malvina the other bedroom. As soon as Orv was asleep, Gord slipped out from under the blankets and walked into the living room.

Mrs. Sheldrake arrived within minutes. Janetta gave her the daily newspaper to read and she left the radio playing in the background.

Gord was excited to drive into the city with Grandpa Ed and Janetta. But mostly, he would get to see Daddy in the hospital—and Orv didn't.

When they reached the intersection of Highway 20 and 56, Grandpa Ed pointed to the right "That's where the new highway is being built. When it's finished, Highway 20 will turn and go down the Stoney Creek Cut and join Highway 8, but today we're taking the old Highway 20 along Rymal Road and Upper Gage." (The Stoney Creek Cut is now called Upper Centennial Parkway.)

Figure 5: The new Stoney Creek Cut was started in 1932.

Grandpa Ed added "You know Gord, your Dad drove a dump truck to bring stones to that new highway."

Gord looked at the new highway with awe and thought to himself "My Dad helped make this ... I'm going to be a truck driver when I grow up."

St. Joseph's Hospital is the biggest building Gord has ever been inside. After walking through a maze of hallways and stairways, they reached a room with four beds.

"That's him," Janetta said as she nudged Gord towards the first bed.

"Hi Daddy," Gord said to wake him.

Gord started to crawl up on the bed, but Janetta quickly pulled him down. "We don't know where his boo boos are."

There were wires and tubes and machines that made a steady noise. Grandpa Ed and Janetta sat down in the two chairs and Gord sat on Janetta's knee.

After a looooong while, Gord asked, "Are we just going to watch him sleep?"

Grandpa Ed smiled. "We're hoping a doctor will come in and tell us how he's doing. Maybe I should go to the nurse's station and see if the doctor is around."

Grandpa Ed returned a short time later and reported that Harry had a broken leg and head injuries. They want him to sleep so his head has a better chance of healing. They continued to watch Harry sleep and eventually headed home so Mrs. Sheldrake could go home.

St. Joseph's Hospital is on Highway 6 in downtown Hamilton, but most people call this section James Street. Grandpa Ed drove the car slowly up the mountain, up Highway 6, until he caught up to a truck trying to climb the mountain. It chugged slowly and at times, it didn't seem to move at all.

On the way home, Grandpa Ed took the original King's Highway 20: Highway 6, turned east onto Concession, south onto Upper Gage Street, and east on Rymal Road, and Highway 20 to Fulton. Before 1930, people referred to it as the Upper Mountain Highway.

"Wow! Look at their gasoline price," Grandpa Ed broke the silence as they drove past a store with a gas pump, "they're selling gas for ten cents a gallon!"

"Is that more than yours?" Janetta asked.

"Yes," Grandpa Ed answered, "I should raise my price."

"I can't believe how much prices are going up. I'm glad I bake my own bread; can you imagine paying seven cents for a loaf of bread?!" Janetta asked.

That's how the conversation went the rest of the way home.

As soon as they walked into the store, Grandma Malvina looked up and asked, "How is Harry?"

"Sleeping," Gord replied, "just sleeping."

"It's not good," Grandpa Ed said, "they don't know what else they can do." He was referring to the doctors in the hospital.

Grandma Malvina reported that she telephoned Edna, Harry's younger sister. As soon as her husband Jack comes home from work, they are going to drive from Binbrook to Fulton, pick her up, and go to the hospital. It will probably take half an hour to get here, the roads being what they are. Some roads are paved, some are stone, and some are still dirt. And not everyone has a car; you can still see horses and carriages, or Bennett buggies: a car pulled by a horse!

"Nettie, do you mind looking after her two kids Wilfred and Bernice tonight?" Grandma asked Janetta.

"No, that's better than taking them to the hospital." Janetta replied, "Come on Gord," Janetta said, "let's go upstairs to see Mrs. Sheldrake, Orv, and Bob."

Orv must have heard them talking because he was waiting at the top of the stairs. Janetta hugged him and picked Bob up off the floor, while Gord sang, "I saw Daddy! I saw Daddy! I went for a ride in the car and we went to the city! And we went in a big, big hospital!"

"Ahhh," Orv whined, "me go."

Janetta thanked Mrs. Sheldrake for looking after the boys and then Grandpa Ed drove her home.

"I'm going to make some dinner," Janetta announced as she laid Bob back down on the blanket on the floor, "Gord, can you play with Orv and Bob?"

Malvina came up from the store and showed Janetta an article in today's newspaper. While Janetta read the newspaper story, Grandma took out a plate.

"Twenty!" Janetta suddenly burst out, "He's twenty-seven years old, not twenty!"

Malvina piled some dinner on the plate and took it downstairs to Ed who was now looking after the store. When Malvina came back upstairs, the rest of the family sat down to dinner: Janetta fed Bob in the wooden highchair, and Malvina, Orv and Gord ate at the table.

Shortly after dinner, Edna arrived with her husband Jack and their two children: Wilfred who's three and Bernice, who just turned one. Jack held Bernice's hand outside as he talked to Ed, while Edna took Wilfred into the shed behind the store to use the outhouse.

"Gord," asked Grandpa Ed, "can you run upstairs and tell Grandma that Edna's here?" Gord went in the store and yelled "Grandma, Aunt Edna's here!"

YOUTH WAS HIT
BY MOTOR CAR

Harry Fanson, Grimsby,
Injured Last Evening

From Our Own Correspondent

Grimsby, April 10—Harry Fanson, 20-year-old son of Edward Fanson, who operates the Fulton general store on No. 20 highway, sustained a fractured left leg, head lacerations and possible internal injuries about 10:30 last night when hit by a motor car in charge of Frank Hopper, 1044 King street east, Hamilton. This injured lad was attended by Dr. Leeds of Smithville, and later removed to St. Joseph's hospital at Hamilton. According to the information given the Spectator reporter at the scene, a car in charge of Bill Bugle, 3234 Yonge street, Toronto, was in front of the Fulton store getting gasoline and a short distance behind it, but also on the driveway off the pavement was a motorcycle in charge of Charlie Spencer, R.R. No. 2, St. Ann's. Young Fanson stood in the driveway talking to Spencer when a west bound car in charge of the Hamilton driver came along and it is alleged suddenly swerved off the pavement to the right of the parked motorcycle, struck Fanson, throwing him over the left fender, and then continued around the driveway narrowly missing Mr. Fanson, sen., and smashing into the Bugle car which was considerably damaged on the left side of the pavement, and then back to the north side where it stopped. Mr. Hopper, the driver, claimed that an eastbound car was approaching him on the wrong side of the road and that he swerved to avoid a head-on collision. The highway was slippery at the time and a light rain was falling.

Provincial Constable W. A. Smith of Grimsby, was called to the scene and made an investigation.

The Hamilton Spectator
Monday, April 10, 1933

Jack, Edna, and Malvina drove to the hospital to visit Harry, but Edna's children Wilfred and Bernice stayed with Janetta, Gord, Orv, and Bob. Grandpa Ed stayed downstairs in the store. If the store is quiet, he'll read a daily newspaper such as the Hamilton Daily Spectator or the Hamilton Herald or the weekly East Hamilton News. But tonight, he had to run the store and pump gas without his son Harry to help him.

Upstairs, Gord showed Wilfred a ball he had found in the ditch last week. Gord, Wilfred, and Orv sat on the floor and rolled it back and forth. Bob creeps over and tries to get it, but they played Monkey in the Middle. Even Bernice wants to play with the ball, but she is a new walker and bending over to pick up the ball is not easy.

"How about I tell you all a story?" Janetta said after a few minutes. She picked Bob up off the floor and sat down in the middle of the couch. Orv and Gord raced over to the couch so they could sit beside their Mom. Wilfred and Bernice were the last to join in. Janetta suggested that Bernice should sit next to her because she is younger than Gord. Sometimes, Gord hates being the oldest.

"Once upon a time, there were three little pigs," Janetta started to recite the story she had told them many times before.

When Janetta finished telling the story, she announced "I think it is time for Bob and Bernice to go to sleep." She stood up, still holding Bob.

"Are they staying over night?" Gord asked.

"No, but it could be late when their Mom returns," Janetta answered. She took Bob into her bedroom, changed his diaper, and laid him in the crib. She was going to come and get Bernice, but Bernice had waddled into the bedroom behind them.

Gord was showing Wilfred his book called The Story of the Three Bears. "Once upon a time, Papa Bear, Mama Bear, and Baby Bear sat down to eat breakfast. They were eating porridge," Gord couldn't really read, but he's heard the story so many times, he knows what happens next. Then, he turned the page so they could see the next picture.

Janetta came into the living room, sat down on the sofa, and listened to Gord's story. When he finished 'reading' the book, she announced, "I'll change Orv into pajamas and put him into bed. Then, I'll take you two outside one more time." She disappeared with Orv into the bedroom.

When Janetta came back into the living room, Gord and Wilfred followed her down the stairs and into the store. "We're going to the outhouse one more time," she said to Grandpa Ed as they passed through the store, "would you mind listening at the bottom of the stairs?" They went out to the shed behind the store.

"Good night, Grandpa," Gord said as they walked back through the store. They went up the stairs and into Janetta's bedroom. Bernice was already asleep in Janetta and Harry's double bed. She tucked Wilfred into bed beside Bernice. Then, Gord went to his bedroom and got in the double bed next to Orv.

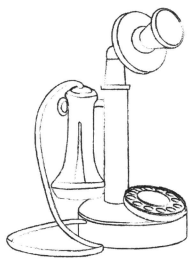

Figure 6: A candlestick telephone used in 1933.

Tragedy on the Twenty

Growing up without a father

It was very quiet while they ate their porridge the next morning. "When is Daddy coming home?" Gord broke the silence.

Janetta looked up from her porridge and replied, "We don't know ... when he wakes up."

"Why doesn't he just come home and sleep here?"

Grandma Malvina—who had been mixing up something in a bowl—stopped and looked up. "I guess when the automobile hit your Dad it hurt his tummy and then he fell down and hit his head."

"We have to wait for all his injuries to get better," Janetta added.

"I miss Daddy," Gord said, "I wish he were here."

"I miss him, too," Janetta said as she reached over to put her arm around him.

Grandma Malvina came closer to the table. "How about we all say a prayer?"

Everyone bowed his or her heads as Grandma Malvina started to pray, "Dear God. Please watch over Harry— Dad—and help his tummy and head to get better. Please bring him home to us soon. Also, give us strength and patience. Amen."

After the boys were washed up and dressed, Grandma Malvina gave Gord a plate with a freshly baked muffin on it and asked him to take it downstairs to Grandpa.

"Here Grandpa," Gord said as he went down the stairs and entered the store, "Grandma made you a muffin."

"Oh, good," Grandpa said as he looked up from the newspaper, "I could use a snack."

"What's in the news today?" Gord asked. He didn't really care, but he knew Grandpa Ed liked talking to people about things he saw in the newspaper.

"It says here that some new immigrants didn't have a job so they got sent back to their own country," he answered.

"What's an immi ..."

"An immigrant is a person who wasn't born in Canada but moved here because they wanted to live here."

"Are we immigrants?" Gord asked slowly.

"No, you were born upstairs," Grandpa Ed smiled, "and I was born in Canada, too. Near Stratford. But, my father was born in England and moved here when he was very young."

"You have a father?" Gord asked, not realizing he had one.

"No. He died before I was born, so I didn't know him," Grandpa Ed said, "but his name was John Fanson. He was gored by a bull."

"He was a bullfighter!" Gord lit up with his eyes wide open.

"No," Grandpa Ed chuckled, "he had a farm with cows and a bull. They had six children and me on the way. But one day, the bull turned suddenly and cut my dad in the stomach with his horn."

"Ooh," Gord curled up my nose, at the grotesque way to die.

"My pregnant mother Mary and the two youngest girls went to live with my Grandmother in Exeter," he went on, "the other children got separated and were raised by other families."

"That's really sad," Gord commented, "no wonder you don't talk about them."

"I know that two girls went out west," Grandfather added, "but I never met them. But, I do have a photo," he added as he took a box off the shelf and fumbled through several old photos. He held up a photo—a studio photo of four girls that was mounted on a card.

"Do you want to go out west and meet them?" Gord asked.

He shrugged his shoulders, "I wouldn't know what to say. We were raised separately. But, I do have a sister in Grimsby."

"So, you grew up without a father?" Gord realized.

"No," Grandpa explained, "I didn't grow up with *my* father, but my mother remarried a man from Welland who had a daughter. Her mother had died. He was my stepfather and he was good to me. And then my mom and him had three more children together."

"I'm glad I have a father," Gord remarked as an automobile drove up to the gas pump. Gord followed Grandpa Ed outside. Grandpa Ed walked over to the driver of the car, while Gord went to play in the dirt pile beside the store. As he started to play with the wooden truck, he realized he hadn't played with it since Daddy's accident. "I hope Daddy wakes up soon," Gord thought to himself, "and maybe he'll take me for a ride in the big dump truck again."

Harry Dies in the Hospital

Janetta was awoken at 4:30 a.m. by the ring of a telephone. Though the telephone was downstairs in the store, she could hear the distinct ring. It also sounded like Grandpa Ed running through the hall, down the stairs, and into the store. Janetta got out of bed and went into the hallway. Grandma Malvina and Gord had also heard the ring and were waiting in the living room, wondering who would be calling so early in the morning.

After a few minutes, Grandpa Ed came back upstairs. "That was the hospital." He just shook his head no and tried hard to control his emotions. "Harry didn't make it." That was not the news they were waiting to hear. Janetta stepped back, hitting the wall as if she wanted it to hold her up.

"I can't believe it," Grandma Malvina said as she looked at Janetta, "not Harry."

"What about the boys?" Janetta asked, "And the baby?" She buried her head in her hands and started to cry. She slid down the wall and sank to the floor.

"I think that's the first time I ever saw her cry," Gord thought to himself. He put his arm around her, "Don't cry Mommy." Then she held him so tight, she squeezed tears out of him. And soon they were all crying.

Grandpa Ed put his hand on her shoulder, "You know we'll help you anyway we can."

Janetta stood up, blew her nose, and nodded, "Thank you." Then she looked at Gord, "You're very sweet, Gord."

"But, young man," Grandpa Ed said, "you should be in bed." Grandpa Ed took Gord into his bedroom and tucked him into bed. It was hard to fall back to sleep; he could hear mumblings in the living room and the occasional sobs.

When Gord got out of bed later in the morning, Orv was already up and sitting at the kitchen table. Janetta gave a spoon of porridge to Orv and then a spoon to Bob, the baby. Grandma Malvina went over to the stove and scooped out some porridge for Gord.

VICTIM OF CRASH DIES IN HOSPITAL

Question of Inquest Being Considered To-day

From Our Own Correspondent

Grimsby, April 12—Harry Fanson, who was struck by a car driven by Frank Hopper, 1044 King street east, Hamilton, on Sunday night, outside his father's general store at Fulton, on No. 20 highway, passed away about 4 o'clock this morning in St. Joseph's hospital.

Twenty-Seven Years Old

Harry Lewis Fanson is the only son of Edward and Mrs. Fanson, of Fulton. He was born in Hamilton and was 27 years of age. He had lived in Fulton for the last nine years and was a member of the United church.

Those who survive are: His wife (formerly Miss Tweedle, of Fulton); three children, Gordon Harry, four years; Orville Stanley, two year; Robert Lewis, nine months; his mother and father, one sister Mrs. Jack Leggatt, of Binbrook. Funeral arrangements have not yet been completed.

Provincial Constable Smith is in St. Catharines today consulting with Coroner Lancaster on the advisability of holding an inquest.

The Hamilton Spectator
Wednesday, April 12, 1933

Janetta seemed to be walking around in automatic pilot. She's wasn't talking much and seemed to be deep in thought.

"What did Grandpa mean when he said 'Daddy didn't make it?'" Gord asked to break the silence.

Janetta looked over at me, "It was a bad accident ... he didn't survive."

"What do you mean?"

"He's not going to wake up," Janetta choked out the words as she shook her head. Tears started flowing like a waterfall down her cheeks.

Gord thought, "That's the second time I've seen Mommy cry." He got down from his chair and walked over to Janetta and put his little arms around her. Then Orv, copying his older brother, got down, walked over and hugged her, too.

A few minutes later, Grandpa Ed came up the stairs from the store. "Gord, you have to eat a little faster," he instructed him.

Grandpa Ed took a deep breath and exhaled rather heavily.

"Did you put up the sign?" Grandma Malvina asked.

"You know I rarely close the store, but I think we should just for today. I have a few telephone calls to make," Grandpa Ed said.

A few minutes later, Grandpa Ed added, "Today is Wednesday. Friday is Good Friday and all the other stores will be closed. We need to re-open tomorrow, Thursday ... just for one day."

"I'll watch the boys if you want to change Bob," Grandma Malvina offered to Janetta.

"Yeah," Janetta mumbled in her trance. She had finished feeding Bob. She wet a cloth and robotically wiped his face and hands, and carried him away into her bedroom.

"Grandpa, Janetta and I need to discuss some things," Grandma told Gord and Orv, "so we need you three to play quietly in the living room this morning." She took the older two boys into the bedroom and dressed them in play clothes.

Soon, they were all dressed and headed into the living room. Grandpa had piled some boxes, blankets, the stuffed bear, and the toy dump truck in the living room.

The grown-ups went into the kitchen and sat down at the kitchen table. Such an ordinary thing—that kitchen table—but so many decisions are made while sitting at it. It's probably the most important piece of furniture in the house … so many discussions, meals, and work are done while sitting at the kitchen table.

"We could have a small funeral here on Saturday afternoon," Grandpa started the conversation.

"Funeral!" Gord thought to himself. He could hear them talking. "That's for dead people. That mean's Daddy's dead … forever."

"Do you want to call the minister, Nettie?" Grandpa Ed asked Janetta.

"I think I can," Janetta replied, "It's the boys. It's hard to do serious things and keep an eye on them, too."

"I can stay up here with the boys, while you go downstairs and telephone the minister," Grandma offered.

"And ask him how much plots are at the church." Grandma added. Well, that opened up the floodgates and the sobbing started uncontrollably. Gord could hear his Mommy crying in the kitchen and he couldn't help himself; a tear trickled down his cheek. He's never heard his mom cry like this before.

Gord walked into the kitchen and put his arms around his mommy. She started crying harder on his shoulder. Soon, there were no dry eyes in the kitchen.

After a while, Janetta stopped crying and blew her nose. "I'm fine now. You go back into the living room and look after Bob," she instructed.

"Nettie, you know my sister Melissa Hartwell, who lives in Grimsby?" Grandpa asked

"And she's married to George? Yes, I've met her," Janetta replied.

"Well, she and George bought two plots at the Queen's Lawn Cemetery in Grimsby and she got a good price for them. So, Malvina and I are going to be buried there, too. Do you want me to get four plots for you?" Grandpa asked.

"Four? You mean Harry and I and only two children?" Janetta asked.

"Well, once they get married, they can be buried wherever they want. If you don't use the two plots, you can sell them."

"Well," Janetta thought aloud, "if you don't mind getting them for me. I can pay for them."

After a few telephone calls, the funeral was planned for Saturday, April 15 at 1:30 in Grandpa Ed and Grandma Malvina's apartment above the store. The funeral is on the Saturday between Good Friday and Easter Sunday.

"I'll drive to Grimsby and see if we can get you four plots near our two plots," he replied.

Grandpa Ed returned home at noon from the Queen's Lawn Cemetery in Grimsby. For $60, Nettie will get four cemetery plots. It will cost $5 to open and close a plot for Harry, and an additional cost of $1.50 for the yearly care.

That night, Grandpa Ed put Gord and Orv to bed because Janetta was busy on the telephone. "I'm not feeling very creative and I don't feel like telling a story. But, I will say something," he continued, "I never want you two to drink and drive."

Gord looked at Orv. They both looked bewildered. "Don't drink milk and drive?" Gord asked.

Grandpa Ed couldn't help but laugh. "No, alcohol. Don't drink liquor and then drive a car," he continued, "that jerk in the car that hit your Dad had a few drinks and then lost control of his car. I would be very disappointed in you if I heard you drank too much and then drove a car."

"I won't," Gord promised Grandpa, "I'm not going to drive a car, I'm going to drive a big truck like Daddy."

"Me too," echoed Orv.

Newspaper Article

Gord was coloring a picture in a coloring book on the floor of the store. Grandma is upstairs with Orv and Bob. Janetta has been on the telephone quite a bit this morning. Grandpa Ed is reading the newspaper when he says out loud "Darn, the New York Rangers won the Stanley Cup last night in overtime. They beat the Toronto Maple Leafs 1-0 to win three games in the play-offs."

"Daddy likes the Maple Leafs. They won the Stanley Cup last year," Gord said.

"Yes, it was his favorite team," Grandpa Ed agreed.

Grandpa Ed was reading the newspaper when he spotted Harry's name in a death notice. Janetta, who had been talking on the telephone, looked over his shoulder at the newspaper, while Grandpa Ed read it aloud.

> ### Deaths
> **FANSON**--At St. Joseph's hospital, on Wednesday, April 12, 1933, Harry L. Fanson, only son of Edward and Mrs. Fanson, of Fulton, aged 27 years. The funeral will take place Saturday, April 15, at the home of his parents, Fulton, with service at 1:30. Interment in Queen's Lawn Cemetery, Grimsby.
> *The Hamilton Spectator*
> *Thursday, April 13, 1933*

"You didn't mention that he had a wife and three boys," Janetta commented.

"Well, I thought you were going to run your own," Grandpa Ed replied, "and it's just a notice of the funeral, if anyone wants to come."

Just then, a motorcycle pulled off the highway and headed up to the store. The driver shut off the motor and took off his helmet and goggles. He looked like an airplane pilot with those goggles. Gord recognized him. He was here the night of the accident. It's Charlie.

Charlie entered the store and looked at Gord. "Are you Harry's son?" he asked him.

"Yes," Gord replied quietly.

"I heard what happened. I am so sorry to hear about your Dad."

Gord didn't know what to say, so he just nodded to acknowledge that he heard him.

"Do you know you look like an airplane pilot when you wear those goggles?"

Charlie laughed, "And I feel like a pilot when I am soaring down the highway, almost as if I am flying! Do you want to go for a ride on my motorcycle?"

Gord looked at Grandpa Ed. "I think we've had enough excitement this week," Grandpa said.

Charlie turned to Grandpa Ed, "I read in the newspaper that he didn't make it ... I'm so sorry. I'm sure they did all they could do."

"Yeah, thanks," Grandpa Ed replied.

"Have you heard from the police yet? Was he charged with anything?" Charlie asked.

"I haven't heard anything yet. I hope so ... for the pain he put Harry through. He just drove fast through the parking lot as if he were still on the highway."

"Yeah, I'm lucky he didn't hit me. I was just two feet away from him."

"I know. He side-swiped customer Bill's car while I was putting gas in it."

"We're all lucky ... it could have been a lot worse."

Charlie left the store, put on his helmet and goggles, and then gave a thumb's up to Gord, who was looking out the window. He sat on the motorcycle, and with a kick, started it up. With a nod, he drove away.

Another car drove into the parking lot. Gord recognized Bennett, who was here on the weekend with the Bennett-mobile. Harry gave him gas in exchange for new shoes.

"Hi," he said to Gord, as he entered the store.

"Hi Bennett," Gord said quietly.

"My name's not Bennett, it's John," he extended his hand to Gord to shake.

"Well, Daddy said you drove a Bennett-mobile," Gord said.

He laughed. "Yes, I guess I did, but it's more comfortable than a horse and buggy."

Then he knelt down on one knee so he was at Gord's eye level. "I am so sorry to hear about your Dad." An awkward silence followed, because Gord didn't know what to say.

"Remember all the good times you and your Dad had; don't remember how he died," he added. Gord nodded to show that he understood, but he wasn't sure that he did.

Then Bennett—John—turned to Grandpa Ed and extended his sympathies.

"By the way, this is Harry's wife Nettie," he introduced Janetta to John. Grandpa Ed explained that John got gas on Sunday before the accident happened.

"I am so sorry for your loss," John said.

"Thank you," Janetta replied.

April 13 was the saddest, yet busiest day in the store. Several families in the area had heard of Harry's passing and stopped into the store with their condolences. Some brought casseroles, homemade bread, desserts, or soup. Some just wanted to come in and show their support.

Later in the afternoon, Grandpa Ed took Gord to Sammy Madger's General Dry Goods Store in Smithville to buy a new shirt for the memorial service on Saturday. Orv will wear one of Gord's old shirts. Sammy Madgers recognized Grandpa Ed when they entered the store and came over.

"Hi Ed. I am so sorry to hear about Harry," he extended his sympathy to Grandpa Ed. "He was a hard worker and a good person."

"Thanks," Grandpa Ed said, "this is his oldest son Gord." Sammy Madger extended his hand to Gord and they shook hands.

"He needs a new shirt for the service," Grandpa Ed added.

"He looks like a size 4," Sammy guessed as he scurried behind a table piled high with clothes. He pulled out a light blue dress shirt and held it up to Gord. Grandpa and Sammy agreed that it was the right size. Grandpa looked at the tag to see the price.

"It's on me," Sammy said to Grandpa.

Grandpa looked surprised and grateful. "Thank you, thank you very much."

Figure 7: Harry Fanson with oldest child Gordon in 1930.

A Day to Remember

"It said in today's newspaper that Bonnie and Clyde survived another shootout with police on Thursday," Grandpa Ed said to a group of neighbors who were gathered around.

"I read that," added Mr. Young. "They got away but they left behind some photographs and evidence." A hundred people were mingling inside and outside the store for Harry's Memorial Service on the Saturday between Good Friday and Easter. The service was scheduled to start at 1:30 p.m., but many people had already arrived an hour before the service.

Grandma Malvina squeezed her way through the crowd of family and friends and whispered to Grandpa Ed "There's no way all these people are going to fit into our apartment."

"I know," Grandpa Ed agreed, "I think we're going to have to announce family only for the actual service upstairs." Grandma Malvina agreed.

Well before 1:30 p.m. on Saturday, Grandpa Ed's apartment above the store was packed with people. Grandpa Ed and Grandma Malvina were greeting people downstairs, while Janetta and the Church Minister were talking to people upstairs.

At 1:30 p.m. Grandpa Ed and Grandma Malvina squeezed through a maze of people and stood on the bottom steps of the stairs that led to the apartment where Harry was resting in peace. "Hello," Grandpa Ed said in his loudest voice. "I want to thank everyone for coming and showing your support to Malvina, Nettie, and our family during this difficult time," Grandpa Ed spoke loudly. "You can stay and mingle if you wish. There's a fresh pot of tea and coffee on the counter. And lots of cookies and cake made by several neighbors. Unfortunately, our small apartment cannot accommodate all of you and we will have to restrict the funeral to immediate family only. After the service, we will be driving to Grimsby to the Queen's Lawn Cemetery. Thank you for coming." Then, he and Grandma made their way upstairs for the funeral.

Once upstairs, they found chairs at the front of the living room near Harry's coffin and sat down. Grandpa Ed, Grandma Malvina, and Janetta were wearing their Sunday-best clothes. Orv was wearing Gord's hand-me-down shirt and sitting on Janetta's knee while Gord—wearing his new blue shirt that Sammy Madgers gave him—sat on Grandpa's knee. Nine-month-old Bob was napping in the bedroom.

Gord looked at the man in the coffin. It kind of looked like his Dad, but different. He was wearing his Sunday-best suit that he only wears to church or weddings. As Gord's eyes made their way down the suit to his shoes, he saw the new shiny black shoes that he got from Bennett. One of the last noble acts of kindness Harry did before the accident.

During the funeral service, Gord stood up and looked around. There sure were a lot of people in their home. Some were standing at the back and in the hall leading to the bedrooms. Several more were standing in the kitchen straining to hear the service. He recognized several aunts and uncles and a few very close friends.

After several speeches, songs, and prayers, Grandpa stood up and made another announcement, "Thank you all for coming today. Thank you everyone who brought cookies or cake. We will stay for a half-hour or so and have tea, coffee, or home-baked goodies with you, and then, we'll be driving to the Queen's Lawn Cemetery in Grimsby. Thank you for joining us today; it means a lot to us."

Then, everyone stood up, stretched, and filed into the kitchen for a drink or munchies.

"Did you hear the hockey game on the radio?" Gord heard Uncle John ask a group of people gathered around him.

"No, but I read it in today's newspaper. New York beat Toronto by one point in overtime!" replied Uncle Anson.

"And they won the Stanley Cup," said Uncle John.

"Well," Uncle Anson continued, "there's always next year."

Gord wandered around the herd of legs and feet until someone would spot him and say, "They were sorry for his loss" or something like that. "Thank you" is what Grandpa Ed said he should say. Gord spotted Orv near the kitchen door and waded over to him as if he were swimming through a sea of legs.

"Come on Orv, let's play a game," Gord said when he reached him. "Pretend we're swimming through this sea of people and we have to make it to land over by the hallway." Orv was game so they made their way through the scores of relatives. Then they swam into to the kitchen. Gord spotted homemade molasses cookies on the counter. If he stands on his tiptoes he can just reach the plate of cookies. He took two—one for Orv and one for him. Soon, there was evidence around Orv's mouth, which Gord knew he had to get rid of. He licked his fingers and wiped around Orv's face, until the crumbs were gone.

Gord heard Grandpa thanking people for coming and realized they were starting to leave. The sea of people was flowing down the stairs and into the store. When it looked like everyone but immediate family was gone, they put on their coats. Janetta went into the bedroom and got Bob out of his crib. They all went downstairs and through the store. There were just a few neighbors remaining and they all went outside.

A black hearse was parked outside in front of the store, with Grandpa Ed's car behind it, and Aunt Edna's car lined up behind it. Grandpa Ed took Gord's hand and they stood beside Janetta, who was holding Bob. Grandma scooped up Orv and held him up so he could see. The minister came out of the store and stood at the back of the hearse. Six men carried the coffin down the stairs, through the store, and out the door. Harry's five brothers-in-laws and an uncle had the honor of carrying the casket. After one more prayer, the coffin was loaded into the back of the hearse and the lines of people dispersed into their cars.

Aunt Edna asked Gord if he wanted to sit with Wilfred in their car to go to Grimsby. He looked at Janetta, but it was Grandpa who said, "Go ahead." Gord smiled as he got in the backseat of Aunt Edna's car with Wilfred. It will be fun riding in a car with a friend—someone his own age.

About seven cars followed the hearse down the mountain into Grimsby. There was a short service and prayer on the grass beside Harry's cemetery plot. After the service, Grandpa pointed to where he and Grandma Malvina will be buried someday—but not for a long time. One day, the family will be together again. *Together.*

The Inquest into Harry's Death

Soon after Harry's funeral, Grandpa Ed and Janetta contacted the law firm of F. R. Murgatroyd, which had offices in Hamilton and Smithville. Grandpa lost his only son and a valuable employee in the car accident. Janetta had lost her husband, the breadwinner of the family, and father of her three—soon to be four—children. She needed to file for support. All of her children were younger than three-and-a-half years of age.

INQUEST INTO FANSON DEATH

Will Make Announcement of Time and Place

From Our Own Correspondent

Grimsby, April 17—Provincial Constable W. A. Smith stated definitely last night than an inquest would be held in the death of Harry Fanson, of Fulton. Following a preliminary investigation by Coroner Dr. Jordan, of Wellandport at the scene, it was agreed that an inquest was necessary. Time and place of inquest had not been decided upon last night, but it will probably be at Smithville.

The Hamilton Spectator
Monday, April 17, 1933

Every day for several weeks, Grandpa Ed searched the Hamilton Spectator newspaper for word about the inquest into his only son's death. At first, he saw short paragraphs in the newspaper about an inquest coming, but no date. Finally, it was announced. An inquest would be held on April 29, 1933 in the Smithville Village Hall. All witnesses should be there including Doctor Leeds, the investigating police officer, Charlie who rode the motorcycle, customer Bill who drove the car that was getting gasoline, and Grandpa Edward Fanson who was pumping gasoline into a vehicle.

Will Hold Inquest Into Fanson Death on Friday

From Our Own Correspondent

Grimsby, April 21 — The inquest into the death of Harry Fanson, of Fulton, who died recently as a result of injuries sustained when hit by a motor car allegedly in charge of Frank Hopper, of Hamilton, will be held in the Smithville village hall on April 23, at 3 p.m.

The Hamilton Spectator
Friday, April 21, 1933

Grandma said she could look after the Fulton store while Grandpa Ed and Janetta went to the inquest, but they would need someone to babysit the boys. Grandpa arranged to drop off the boys at Aunt Edna's house in Binbrook to play with her two children.

Once the inquest into Harry's death got started, it was Dr. Leeds of Smithville who spoke first. He received a telephone call around 10:30 p.m. on Sunday, April 9 telling him there had been an automobile accident at the Fulton Store. He estimated it took about 20 minutes to put on his coat and drive to Fulton. It was very dark in front of the store, but he observed that Harry was in a great deal of pain and lying on the gravel. There was a wet towel on his forehead. "I could tell by the way his leg was laying that it was broken," Dr. Leeds testified. He went on to explain how they put a splint on his leg to stabilize it and then he and Harry's father lifted Harry into the backseat of the car. He took Harry and his wife Janetta Fanson to St. Joseph's Hospital in Hamilton.

Dr. Ballantyne listed all of Harry's injuries that were consistent with someone who had just been hit by a motor vehicle: head injuries, leg injuries, and the beginning of bronchio-pneumonia. He had ruled the cause of death to be head and leg injuries.

The lawyer representing the Fanson family asked Provincial Constable Smith, the police officer several questions pertaining to his investigation of the scene. Had he measured the distance the accused's car had travelled before coming to a stop? Had he noticed any odd behavior by the accused?

"Do you think the accused had been drinking prior to the accident?" asked the lawyer.

"There was no sign of intoxication or liquor on the accused," Smith replied.

"That's a lie!" blurted out Grandpa Ed Fanson who suddenly rose from his seat.

"Please sit down. I will not have any outbursts at this inquest" said the judge presiding over the inquest.

Charlie Spencer, the motorcycle driver was then called to the stand. He lived in Bismarck, but had stopped at the Fulton General Store to get gas. He was sitting on his motorcycle but it wasn't running. He was about one foot from the King's Highway 20. Harry Fanson was standing about two feet away. They were talking while Charlie waited to get gas. Then, suddenly a car went off the highway and into the gravel parking lot of the store. It hit Harry and sent him flying over the left fender of the car, hit the left side of a car that was getting gas, and then came to a stop on the other side of the lot. He couldn't guess how fast the car was traveling. He did not see any other cars on the highway at that time.

Next, customer Bill Bugle told his recollection of the evening of Sunday, April 9, 1933. He lived in Toronto, but at the time of the accident, he was standing outside his vehicle as Edward Fanson was pumping gas into it. He saw the Hopper car hit Harry Fanson, sideswipe the left side of his car, and then come to a stop on the other side of the gravel parking lot.

The car was traveling "swiftly," Bill replied when asked to estimate the speed of Hopper's car when it hit Harry.

Then Bill described a conversation he had after the accident with Miss Hopper, who was in the Hopper car at the time of the accident. He recalled her words as being: "There were a lot of lights. They dazzled me, and I couldn't see, and then mother said, 'You've hit a car.'"

It was Grandpa Edward Fanson who provided the most detail about the accident. While he was waiting for Dr. Leeds to arrive, he counted paces from where his son Harry Fanson was laying to where the Hopper car came to a stop. He estimated about 122 feet. The Hopper car had to be traveling fast because it couldn't stop right away after hitting Harry.

"How fast do you think the Hopper car was traveling?"

"The car must have been traveling at 60 or 70 miles an hour," Grandpa Ed explained.

"Just like a flash of lightning is how it went," he told the coroner. "He didn't slow down when he came into the gravel parking lot ... he drove fast as if he were still on the highway."

"Perhaps, if the police had measured the distance it took for the car to stop, you'd see he was traveling too fast to stop when he saw Harry. He went another 122 feet!" implying that the police had not made a satisfactory examination of the accident.

"He also didn't test the driver to see that he had been drinking!" Grandpa Ed said getting louder with each statement.

A few other people who came by after the accident gave testimony before it was Frank Hopper's turn to sit at the front of the inquiry. He drove the out-of-control car.

"There was a light drizzle, so I drove carefully, maybe 30—no probably 25—miles per hour," said Hopper. He also told how his car was in good working condition and that both his headlights and brakes were working that night.

"Did the police officer check your headlights to make sure both were working?" asked the lawyer representing the Fanson family.

"No," Hopper replied.

"Did the police officer drive your car to make sure the brakes were working properly?"

"No, but I drove home that night and they worked fine."

"Well then, what happened that night?"

"Lights seemed to flash all over the highway. I swung to the right to clear. It looked like two or three cars." Hopper explained, "I didn't see Fanson at all, and didn't know I had hit him until I walked back. I didn't use my brakes at all during the whole affair."

Grandpa Edward Fanson stood up and yelled "You didn't see a man standing in front of you?! Were you even paying attention?!"

"Order," demanded the coroner.

At the end of the inquiry, the jury foreman stood up and said "We, the jury empaneled in the case of Harry Fanson find that he came to his death on April 12, from injuries received as the result of an accident on No. 20 highway, in the township of South Grimsby, when he was struck by a motor car owned and driven by Frank Hopper, on the 9th of April, 1933."

But, crown authorities laid no charges against Frank Hopper in connection with the accident. Acting on behalf of the widow of Harry Fanson, F. R. Murgatroyd, of Hamilton entered a suit for unstated damages.

INQUEST HELD IN FANSON ACCIDENT

Struck By Motor Car on Highway 20 on April 9

Hopper Says He Was Driving Carefully

From Our Own Correspondent

Grimsby, April 29—"We, the jury empaneled in the case of Harry Fanson find that he came to his death on April 11, from injuries received as the result of an accident on No. 20 highway, in the township of South Grimsby, when he was struck by a motor car owned and driven by Frank Hopper, on the 9th of April, 1933."

Above is the verdict returned by the jury under Coroner Dr. Graham A. Jordan, of Wellandport, at Smithville yesterday afternoon, on the death of Harry Fanson, of Fulton, who died in St. Joseph's hospital at Hamilton about 3:50 a.m. on April 11 last, following injuries received when struck by a motor car as he stood in the driveway at his father's general store in Fulton on the night of April 9.

Crown Attorney E. H. Lancaster, K.C. of St. Catharines, represented the crown, while F. R. Murgatroyd, of Hamilton, represented the Fanson family.

Dr. J. H. Leeds, of Smithville, testified that he attended Fanson at the scene of accident, and removed him to hospital.

Dr. Elliot N. Ballantyne, of Hamilton, described the findings and gave cause of death as death from head and leg injuries, coupled with beginning of bronchipneumonia.

Provincial Constable Smith, of Grimsby, told of the investigation he had made at the scene following accident. In answer to a direct question from the crown attorney, he stated there was no sign of intoxication or liquor on Mr. Hopper, and his general condition was normal.

Astride Motorcycle

Charles Spencer, of Bismarck, said he was astride his motorcycle two feet south of Fanson when he was hit, and the motorcycle was about one foot from the highway. Fanson was talking to him, and the motorcycle was between Fanson and the traveled part of highway. He could not say if the Hopper car was going fast, slow or normal. He saw no other cars going either east or west at the time of the accident.

Bill Bugle, Toronto optician, whose car was getting gas at the Fanson gas pump, and was sideswiped by the Hopper car after it had hit deceased, gave a clear description of the accident. He saw the Hopper car and Harry Fanson both at the same time, and saw the man struck by the car. He also described how his own car was hit, and where the Hopper car stopped following the accident. Other than saying "swiftly," he was unable to estimate the speed of Hopper's car. He added that he had talked to Miss Hopper following the accident, and while there perhaps might have been a misinterpretation on his part, he recalled her words as being: "There were a lot of lights. They dazzled me, and I couldn't see, and then mother said, 'You've hit a car.'"

Measurements

Edward Fanson, father of deceased, gave measurements taken following the crash, which showed that Hopper's car came to a stop about 122 feet from where the injured man's body lay. He thought the car must have been traveling at 60 or 70 miles an hour. "Just like a flash of lightning is how it went," he told the coroner. He expressed the opinion that the police had not made a satisfactory examination of the accident.

B. Culp, George Krikorian and Arthur Sheldrake, all of Fulton, told of events following accident.

Frank Hopper, 1044 King street east, Hamilton, driver of the car that hit Fanson, testified that he was driving very carefully, owing to weather conditions. His car, he said, was in fair condition, with both brakes and headlights good. "Lights seemed to flash all over the highway. I swung to the right to clear. It looked like two or three cars. I didn't see Fanson at all, and didn't know I had hit him until I walked back. I didn't use my brakes at all during the whole affair. I was going under 30 miles an hour, and when I struck Fanson probably not over 25 miles an hour," he said.

Following were the members of the jury: C. L. Adams, John Hesler, Ed Downs, John Downey, Arthur Lampman, Goodman Pettigrew and H. O. Tuck. John Hesler acted as foreman.

No charges have been laid by crown authorities against Frank Hopper in connection with the accident. Acting on behalf of the widow of Harry Fanson, F. R. Murgatroyd, of Hamilton has entered suit for unstated damages.

The Hamilton Spectator
Saturday, April 29, 1933

An Outpouring of Support

News of Harry Fanson's death spread quickly through the villages of Fulton and Tweedside. The Fulton General Store was a well-known fixture in the area, and everyone knew that Harry was a hard worker. Since his father Edward and mother Malvina bought the store nine years before, neighbors had watched Harry and his sister Edna mature into young adults. Harry was eighteen years old when they moved into the apartment above the store. He was a dump truck driver by day, but worked evenings and weekends at the store.

At twenty, he married Janetta Tweedle, from nearby Tweedside. Janetta's family was well known in the community for helping to build the Tweedside United Church.

And many people felt Janetta's pain. Can you imagine losing your husband with three young boys to look after and another baby on the way—during the depression? There was an emotional outpouring of support from their neighbors. Each day for weeks, families dropped off casseroles or desserts at the store. They provided babysitting services or just offered their condolences. And then there was Clarence McDougall, who made sure Janetta always had apples—picked from his apple orchard in Fulton.

After Harry's death, Janetta hired lawyer F. R. Murgatroyd to represent her. They had offices in Smithville and Hamilton. A few months later, she received compensation from the insurance company, rumored to be $2,500. She arranged to have a new, wood frame house built next to the store. She knew that's what Harry would want her to do. For years, they talked about getting their own house and moving out of his parents' apartment—together. Finally, they would have their own home to raise their children.

On the day that construction was scheduled to begin, Janetta hurried to feed and dress the boys. She wanted to go over to the construction site to see their dream coming true. She knew it would take several weeks for the two men to complete the house. She didn't need a fancy house—just three bedrooms, a living room, and an eat-in kitchen. She didn't need a new outhouse—they could continue to use the one in the shed behind the store. The builders couldn't promise that the house would be finished before her new baby was expected to arrive, but soon afterward. She was just weeks away from her mid-July due date.

After she fed the boys breakfast and got them dressed, Janetta hurried the three boys down the stairs and through the store. With Janetta carrying Bob and holding hands with Orv and Gord, they stepped outside the store. She stopped. Her mouth dropped open. There wasn't two men working on her house next door—there were twenty men! There was a bustle of activity going on: some men were cutting wood, some were hammering, and others had just finished the stone foundation. She stood there for several seconds unable to move. She was shocked at seeing so many people. She spotted her sister-in-law with a plate of home-baked cookies walking around the construction site offering the men a treat.

Janetta and the boys walked across the gravel parking lot to the site of her new home. She was shocked and pleasantly surprised to see all these men working on her house! *Together.* Word had spread that the widow Fanson was building a house next to the store and they wanted to help. She recognized a few of her brothers and other men from the area. And the tears started to flow again. Not sad tears, but happy tears. An overwhelming sense of gratitude swept over her and she suddenly felt weak-kneed, but there was no chair around to sit down. She set Bob down, but held onto his hand. She felt such an overwhelming support from the community. She walked around the construction site and personally thanked each person for taking time out to help her and her sons. The small, wood-frame house just west of the Fulton store was built in days—not weeks.

When they walked back to the store, Janetta took Orv and Bob upstairs, but Gord lingered in the store with Grandpa Ed. He was at the counter reading the newspaper, but looked up when Gord approached.

"It says here that the Prairie Provinces aren't getting enough rain and some of the cows have starved or suffocated," Grandpa Ed read from the newspaper. "Thousands of people have left the area because their crops were withering."

"Withering?" Gord asked.

"Gardens need water to grow, so if they don't get enough water, the plants could dry out and die."

"Like Daddy." Gord said. Grandpa Ed nodded.

Grandpa Ed walked around the counter and kneeled on one knee in front of Gord. "You know Gord," he said as he put his hand on Gord's shoulder, "you're the man of the family now. You should look after your mother as you get older."

"Man of the family?" Gord thought to himself. "I'm only three! I won't be four until October." As he stood there not knowing what to say, he looked at Grandpa Ed. With the sun streaming through the window behind, Gord could see Grandpa Ed's face very clearly. He was fifty-seven years old with dark hair and a mustache. He was just starting to get wrinkles. Gord examined each wrinkle on Grandpa Ed's face; every line tells a story. He's been through a lot lately. He just lost his only son and he's had to remain strong for the whole family. It was him who arranged the funeral, the cemetery, and still had to run the store. He probably misses Harry as much as Gord does.

"I love you Grandpa," Gord said as he leaned forward and hugged him. As Gord held him, he heard a sniff and realized Grandpa Ed was crying. Grandpa Ed picked Gord up and sat him on the counter, never letting go of him. It didn't take long for Gord's own tears to find their way out of his eyes and stream down his face onto Grandpa Ed.

After a few minutes, Grandpa Ed pulled a handkerchief out of his pocket, wiped his eyes, and then wiped Gord's eyes. "You're the man in your family and I'm the man in our family. We have to be strong—*together*." He tried to smile, but it was hard to hide his own pain—and fear.

Four under four

Summer 1933. Baseball and solo airplane flights are in the news. On July 2, "one of the greatest games in the history of baseball" was played when pitcher Carl Hubbell of the New York Giants pitched 18 innings, without walking a single batter in a game with the St. Louis Cardinals. And then on July 6, the first Baseball All-Star Game was played.

On July 8, Amelia Earhart Putnam flew across the United States in 17 hours and 7 minutes to set a new airplane speed record. But Wiley Post left on July 15 to become the first person to fly solo around the world.

On July 18, Janetta Fanson had just put Bob in the crib, and her other two sons in their beds for the evening when she felt the backache coming on. She knew tonight was the night she had anticipated, but also feared.

Janetta already had three boys and was hoping for a girl this time around. How fun it would be to brush her hair and braid it. And buy dresses. She had already narrowed the potential baby names down to two names: Harry if it's a boy or Harriet if it's a girl, after Harry.

Janetta telephoned her mother-in-law Malvina at the Fulton Store to warn her that she had a backache and she felt tonight was the night. Malvina said she would go out to the garden and warn Edward. Grandpa Ed also had a garden behind the store to grow vegetables to sell in the store and for their family to eat. He grew corn, potatoes, beans, carrots, cucumbers, lettuce, and beets. It was nice to have fresh vegetables in the summer, but you also had to preserve some to last through the winter. Most of the cucumbers would be used to make pickles or relish, which could be sold in the store and fed to the family. Grandpa Ed liked fresh cucumber sandwiches, but relish sandwiches will do in the winter. And Malvina's homemade strawberry jam is delicious, too. Some of the beets will be pickled, as well. The potatoes would be stored in the cold shed and should last through most of the winter.

After Grandpa Ed came into the store and washed up, Malvina went upstairs to get the overnight bag she had packed a week ago. She walked next door with her overnight bag to spend the night with Janetta.

After she settled in, Malvina sat at the kitchen table and opened up the newspaper she brought. "I'm reading that in Germany, they created a law that handicapped people are not allowed to have offspring and have to be sterilized! It says that if you have schizophrenia, epilepsy, or you're mentally retarded you have to be sterilized so you can't reproduce."

"That seems a little harsh. Some people with an illness could be fully functioning," Janetta replied.

"I agree." Malvina continued, "But that new Chancellor of Germany ... Adolf Hitler ... I don't trust him ... he's making a lot of changes."

"Have you thought about a name for the baby?" asked Malvina, "since you're not allowed to call it Hitler." Germany had just passed a law forbidding the name Hitler for a baby.

Janetta sat back in the armchair with the hot water bottle. "If it's a girl, I'm going to name her Harriet," she announced. "If it's a boy, I'm going to name him Harry, after the father he'll never..." her voice trailed off as a wave of tears fell down her cheeks and onto her nightie.

"Do you think we should telephone Dr. Leeds and let him know it will be sometime tonight?" Malvina changed the topic. Dr. Leeds has an office in Smithville, but travelled to deliver a baby.

Janetta shrugged her shoulders. "I have a backache but the labor pains haven't started yet."

"Then, let's wait."

Janetta checked to make sure she had enough extra sheets on the bed and towels nearby. She also heated up some water on the stove and poured it into the hot water bottle. Then she slipped into bed with the hot water bottle under her back.

Within hours, they were in full deliver-a-baby-mode. Dr. Leeds and Edward had joined Janetta and Malvina at Janetta's house. Grandpa Edward read the newspaper at the kitchen table, while the other three were in Janetta's bedroom.

"I saw the top of a head, but then it went back," said Dr. Leeds.

"You're doing good, Janetta," Malvina encouraged her.

Another contraction and they both went back to pushing her bent legs forward. As Dr. Leeds saw the head coming out, he let go of Janetta's leg and gently guided the baby out, making sure not to get the shoulders stuck. Then all of a sudden a baby was lying on the bed attached by an umbilical cord. He held the baby by its feet and reached into the mouth to remove mucus. The baby started to cry. And Janetta let out a sigh of relief. It was alive and breathing. He laid it down on Janetta's tummy and reached for two clamps that he had laid on the night table next to the bed. He positioned the two clamps on the umbilical cord and reached for the scissors. "Do you want to do the honors?" he asked Malvina. She took the scissors and with one snip ended the attachment between baby and mother.

"Is it a girl?" Janetta asked as she slid the baby up closer to her chest and took a look at his male parts. "It's a boy," she announced, as tears of happiness mixed with exhaustion flowed down her cheeks.

"Are you still planning to call him Harry?" Malvina asked.

Janetta nodded "Yes, Harry William Fanson."

Figure 8: Son Harry William Fanson turned one in July 1934.

Taking Control

Janetta woke up one morning, put on a robe, and wandered into the kitchen. Aunt Olive was feeding Bob, while Gord and Orv fed themselves at the kitchen table. All three boys were already dressed.

"Hi, Mommy," Gord said as she entered the room.

"Good morning," she replied, "wow, you three are already dressed and eating breakfast."

They beamed with pride.

Janetta's younger brother John Tweedle, his wife Olive, and their baby Marion had moved into one the three bedrooms to help Janetta. He worked on his father's farm in nearby Tweedside. With winter approaching, he was planning to help shovel snow or protect her; Olive had a child to look after so she could help Janetta with her young children, too.

"Do you mind if I take the boys for a walk?" Aunt Olive asked.

Janetta shook her head. "No, I don't mind."

"Good. The babies have been changed and gone back to sleep." Aunt Olive updated her. Janetta knew she was referring to her baby Harry and Aunt Olive's baby Marion.

"OK, let's tidy up your dishes and then we'll go see Grandma." Aunt Olive instructed the boys who carried their empty bowls over to the sink.

She took their coats off the hooks by the front door and put them on the boys.

"You'll watch the babies, right?" Aunt Olive asked as she and the three older boys stepped outside.

"Yes," Janetta replied as she made some fresh coffee.

Within five minutes, Malvina knocked on the door. Janetta invited her in for coffee.

"Is everything okay?" Janetta asked, as she handed Malvina a cup of coffee.

"Yes," Malvina replied, "but I think we need to talk."

Janetta looked up at her, as she sat down at the kitchen table.

"I know you've been through a horrible tragedy and it takes time to mourn his loss," Malvina said, "but you have four wonderful boys who've lost their father—and their mother."

Janetta didn't know what to say ... she was caught off guard ... lost their mother?

"I have tried to be patient and Olive and I don't mind helping you with household chores and looking after the boys, but I think it's time you came home," Malvina continued.

Janetta was at a loss for words, "I ... I..." was all she could get out.

"I know it takes time to grieve, but it's been six months. Your boys have experienced a loss, as well ... you need to get on with your life ... you need to start caring for your boys ... for Harry's boys."

Janetta didn't know how to respond ... she needed all her strength to resist the urge to cry.

"Nettie, if you were reading a best-selling novel, and the heroine had just experienced an insurmountable tragedy, how would you expect the heroine to react?" asked Malvina. "Would she wither up and die? Or would she eventually rise up and take control?"

"But, this isn't a book. This is real life."

"Well then, how do you want your story to end?" Malvina asked, "Their mother had given up so her four children grew up and became the Feared Fanson Four and robbed banks, just like Bonnie and Clyde? Is that really what you want for your boys?"

Janetta took out a handkerchief and blew her nose.

"Nettie, only you can change an unhappily ever after into a happily ever after ... not just for you, but for your boys, too."

"I'm sorry that yours and Harry's dreams have been shattered," Malvina continued. "But you can still carry out your plans without him. You wanted to have children together and you got that. You two wanted your own home and you got that."

Deep down, Janetta knew she was right.

"It's time for you to turn your attention to feeding and caring for your children. Stop feeling sorry for yourself. 'Oh, poor me.'" Malvina continued. "I don't mind helping, but you need to help, too. There are five children in this house all under the age of four ... I don't want to be mean, but I want you to go in your bedroom, get dressed, and then come back in here and wash dishes." Malvina stood up and pointed toward the bedroom.

Janetta didn't stop to reply, because by the tone, she thought she should hurry into the bedroom and get dressed. As she got dressed, she glanced in the mirror. "Maybe, Malvina is right," she thought to herself.

"It's okay to be okay," she said to herself as she washed her face. "Harry's gone and there's nothing I can do or say that will bring him back. But, I can be a better mother to his children."

"That's what I'll do," Janetta resolved, "I have to take back control of my life—my family—and make sure the boys get the best kind of upbringing. Moving on doesn't mean forgetting."

When Janetta came out of the bedroom five minutes later, Malvina was making the boys' bed. Since baby Harry was born, Bob has moved into the double bed with Gord and Orv, while baby Harry sleeps in the crib in Janetta's bedroom. Janetta went into the kitchen and washed the breakfast dishes.

"When are the boys coming home?" Janetta asked Malvina.

She looked at the clock in the living room. "How about you wash the kitchen floor before they get back?" she replied.

Janetta heated up some water in the largest pot on the stove, and then poured it into the steel pail, added a bit of cleanser, and started washing the floor in the kitchen. "She's right," she thought to myself, "I do need to start taking charge. Maybe I needed that kick in the pants to get going."

"It looks good," Malvina remarked. "It's nice to have a new wood floor. At our place, I wash the old floor, but it never really looks any different ... it's still an old floor."

Janetta stood up and admired the shine. "I am probably the only one in Fulton who has a new floor. I'm so glad—and lucky—that so many people helped build this house."

"Yes, you are," agreed Malvina, as she left the room to respond to Harry's cries in the bedroom.

The floor by the stove was dry, so Janetta heated up some of yesterday's soup. The boys were thrilled when they came home to a bowl of homemade soup.

Remembering Harry by the Stream

The next day was a Friday and it was Gord's fourth birthday. Janetta woke up early and decided she was going to celebrate Gord's birthday—and not mourn Harry's passing. Today was the first day of the rest of her life and she was going to live it. She felt rejuvenated as she got dressed in her bedroom and then went into the kitchen to wash her face in the sink. She started to boil water on the wood-burning stove to make porridge.

"Wow, you're up early," Aunt Olive said as she walked into the kitchen.

"Yes," Janetta answered, "yes, I am. Today is Gord's fourth birthday and I'm going to take them for a walk to the stream after breakfast. Do you mind watching Harry?"

"No," Aunt Olive answered, "I'm glad to see you motivated." Aunt Olive's daughter Marion was now a month old, and Janetta's baby Harry was three months old.

After breakfast, Janetta pulled Orv and Bob in a wagon down the dirt road by the store. There wasn't enough room in the wagon for Gord, so he had to walk along side. When they reached the stream, Gord ran towards the stream.

"Don't go too close to the water," Janetta yelled, as she lifted Orv and Bob out of the wagon.

Janetta gathered the boys together. "Do you remember the story Harry told you about finding a baby snapping turtle by the stream? You wanted Daddy to take you to a stream."

"I'm going to pick some wild flowers," Janetta said as she proceeded to pick some blue, white, and yellow wildflowers.

"It's time to say good-bye to one of the best storytellers ever," she said with a slight quiver in her voice. "Daddy may not tell you a story again, or kiss you good night, or build forts out of boxes ... you may not be able to see him, but he is always here to listen to you," she said, desperately trying to stay strong.

"Isn't he ever coming home?" Gord asked.

Janetta blew her nose with the handkerchief she had brought. "No," she answered, "he was just too hurt to get better. You saw him sleeping, but his soul went to heaven ... and maybe he will tell stories there."

Gord squeezed her hand and tried to comfort her. A few minutes later, he said, "I'll tell you stories."

"You're such a sweet boy, Gord," she said, as she kneeled down and hugged him. Orv came over and hugged her from behind. Soon, they were all hugging and crying at the same time.

Janetta blew her nose once more and stood up. "Good-bye Daddy. We miss you." She tossed the bouquet of wild flowers into the stream.

"Bye, Daddy," Gord waved, even though he wasn't sure who or what he was waving to.

"Bye, bye," Orv imitated him and waved good-bye to the flowers, which had started to float down steam.

As she stood there by the stream, Janetta realized that the wrenching pain she had felt, was gone. She still missed Harry and she still felt sad, but the ache had dissipated.

"I have been through the worst experience I could ever imagine, but I've made it ... I feel like I'm on the other side now," Janetta thought to herself. "Maybe Malvina was right. I will—and I did—get through this. *Together*."

One year later

"Did Daddy have blonde hair like Bob or brown hair like me?" Gord asked.

Janetta looked at him and then at Bob and said, "He had brown hair. I don't think Bob's hair will stay blonde. It will probably get darker in a few years like mine."

"You don't remember him much anymore, do you?" Janetta asked him a few minutes later.

"Well, I remember him playing with us and I remember driving his big truck, but I've kind of forgotten exactly what his face looked like."

"I know what you mean, Gord," Janetta said, "I wish I had stopped and listened a little more. I wish I had looked at him when he talked and memorized every feature of his face ... but we had a baby a year after we got married. And then another. And then another. And he was always working ... he worked hard for us ... I wish I had taken more photos of him."

Janetta suddenly snapped her fingers, "That's it! I'll take a picture of all of you boys! I can't take any pictures of your Dad, but I can get a picture of you boys." She seemed genuinely pleased with her idea.

Baby Harry William Fanson celebrated his first birthday on Wednesday, July 18, 1934. Janetta dressed Baby Harry up and put him on a blanket on the front steps of the new house and took a photo. She bought a camera with the insurance money to take pictures of the boys. Of course, she still has to pay for film for the camera and pay to have the film processed and have her black and white photographs printed.

Figure 9: Robert Fanson, 2, and Harry Fanson Jr. 1 in July 1934.

The following Sunday, July 22, Janetta dressed the boys in their Sunday-best clothes and took them to church with Grandpa Ed and Grandma Malvina. Right after lunch, she loaded them into Grandpa Ed's car and he drove them into Smithville. On Sunday afternoons, a professional photographer comes to Merritt's Funeral Home and sets up a temporary studio in the parlor. Since the funeral home didn't operate on Sundays, the photographer could use the room and take portraits of families and individuals.

The photographer put Harry and Robert on a beautiful, carved wooden chair. Orv sat on the arm of the chair, and Gord stood on the other side of the chair. (We discovered that chair during Gord's funeral at Merritt's Funeral Home 72 years later.) Janetta must have been very proud of that photo of her four sons because she ordered four copies!

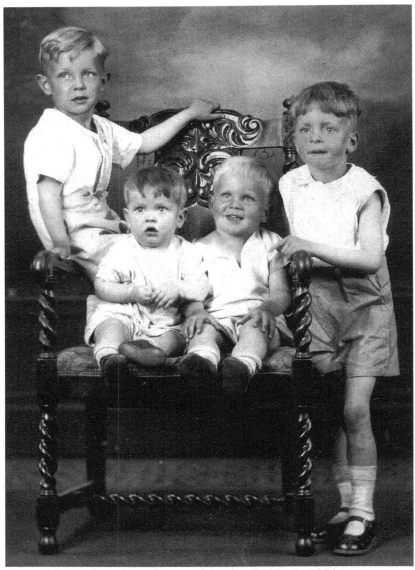

Figure 10: Orval, Harry, Robert, and Gordon Fanson in 1934.

Tragedy on the Twenty

Epilogue

The events of April 9, 1933 changed the lives of many people and shattered so many dreams. Then, and for generations to come.

Two years after that fateful night, Grandpa Edward Fanson had a heart attack and died on June 27, 1935, at the age of 59. He is buried ten feet away from Harry in the Queen's Lawn Cemetery in Grimsby.

Unable to maintain the Fulton Store by herself, Grandma Malvina Fanson sold it and moved in with her daughter Edna Leggett and her family in Binbrook.

Figure 11: Malvina (Doan Fanson) Fell with great-grandchild Janet Fanson in 1953.

Malvina's younger sister Marilla passed away in 1944. On June 29, 1946, Grandma Malvina married her sister's widow Franklin Simcoe Fell (called Frank) in Hamilton. He passed away in 1949 is buried next to his first wife Marilla at Doan's Ridge Cemetery in Welland. At the age of 82, Malvina passed away on July 7, 1960 and is buried next to her first husband Edward Fanson in Queen's Lawn Cemetery in Grimsby.

The Fulton Store still exists, but it has been moved back farther away from Highway 20. Because of the tragic accident and increased traffic on Highway 20, it was determined that the store was too close to the highway and it was moved back, away from the highway. If you stand on Highway 20 and look at the store and the little frame house to the left, the house is closer to the highway than the store. Stanley and Betty Riddiough later bought the Fulton store and renovated the upstairs apartment. The store has had several owners since that tragic day in 1933.

Shortly after the house was built, Uncle John and Aunt Olive Tweedle moved into one of the three bedrooms. John Tweedle is Janetta's younger brother. They were married four days before the April accident. They delivered their first child Marion on September 19, 1933. Marion was two months younger than Janetta's youngest son Harry. Aunt Olive helped a lot around the house changing diapers, preparing meals, and cleaning. Janetta was glad her brother John was staying with them. He provided security but also helped around the house shoveling snow, cutting grass, or painting.

Aunt Olive thought Janetta spent a lot of time in her bedroom crying. Were the tears because she lost her husband or was she suffering from postpartum depression after the birth of her fourth child? No one knows for sure, but one morning Janetta woke up early, got dressed, and was determined not to spend another day feeling sorry for herself. She was the parent of four fine boys and they deserved a "normal" life.

Uncle John and Aunt Olive Tweedle also had dreams of having their own house—together— to raise their growing family. They eventually got their own home in Binbrook and had five children in total.

That first winter without Harry was one of the worst. Not just because Harry was gone and Grandpa Ed Fanson and Uncle John Tweedle had to shovel the snow, but it was the coldest winter on record. Ontario set a record on December 29, 1933 for the coldest day ever: -38.9°C. And the cold wave lasted into February of 1934. Hospitals were jammed with frostbite victims and for the second time in recorded history, Lake Ontario completely froze over.

Janetta was so glad to be in her new, much warmer house. But, she was also stuck indoors with four young boys for months. Occasionally, if Uncle John wasn't shoveling and it wasn't too cold outside, Gord and Orv could go outside and play in the snow. That's when Gord missed his Dad the most. He remembered making a snow fort with his Dad just a month before he died. His Dad dug a tunnel through a snow bank and Gord had to crawl through it to get into the snow fort. The next day, they found rabbit droppings in the snow fort, so they thought a rabbit slept in there.

After Grandpa Ed died, and the Fulton Store was sold, the third bedroom in the little frame house was changed into an indoor washroom with a chemical toilet.

Janetta Fanson never remarried. She raised the four boys in the small, wooden frame house next to the store until the boys had all married and left home. The house still stands beside the store, though it currently has blue, vinyl siding instead of the original clapboard.

Since she couldn't drive an automobile and had four young boys at home, she couldn't go out and get a job. So she started babysitting other people's children in her home, to supplement her social assistance check. Back in 1933, women only took a six-week unpaid break from work when they had a baby, so occasionally Janetta made some extra money by babysitting other people's children.

Once the boys were old enough, they picked fruit during their summer vacation from school, to bring in some extra money. All four boys walked the kilometer from their house next to the Fulton Store to the one-room schoolhouse in Fulton.

After the last son married and moved out, Janetta moved to Hamilton and continued to babysit children. In 1972, Janetta sold one of the four plots she had purchased in 1933 in the Queen's Lawn Cemetery in Grimsby.

Janetta Fanson died in 1992 and is buried next to her husband Harry Louis Fanson and son Robert Lewis Fanson (Bob) in the Queen's Lawn Cemetery in Grimsby, Ontario. When Janetta was buried on October 6, 1992, she still had two sons Gord and Orv, fourteen grandchildren, and twenty-one great-grandchildren.

The oldest son Gordon Harry Fanson completed grade eight at the one-room schoolhouse in Fulton, and then started driving a big truck, just as he promised his Dad. He married Lois Murdock in 1950 and they had six children: Janet Anne, Gordon Edward, Shirley Jean, Patricia Louise, Barbara Ann (the author), and Sandra Lynn. The oldest child was named Janet after her grandmother Janetta. And of course, their son Gordon Edward was named after his father and great-grandfather Ed. They lived in Binbrook, Fulton, but mostly Smithville.

They had a stillborn baby in 1956 and buried him at the foot of his grandfather's grave in Queen's Lawn Cemetery.

Figure 13: In 1950, Gord owned a 1934 Chev.

Orval Stanley Fanson also became a truck driver when he finished school. Orv was the last of the boys to get married and move out of the small frame house in Fulton. He married Irene King and they had three daughters: Terry, Lynda, and Deborah (Debbie). At Orv's funeral in October 1999, his daughter Terry ended her eulogy with a "Ten-Four Yellow Jacket." (Goodbye Yellow Jacket, his handle on a CB radio.)

Robert Lewis Fanson (Bob) grew up and became a truck driver, just like his brothers and father. He died on February 25, 1952 when he was just nineteen years old. He was thrown from a transport truck and hit a tree. A heartbroken Janetta buried him next to his father Harry in the Queen's Lawn Cemetery in Grimsby.

Harry William Fanson, Janetta's youngest son was born three months after his father was killed in the car accident. Like his brothers, he walked to the one-room schoolhouse in Fulton. But, he was able to take a school bus to the Smithville High School, to further his education. He, too, became a truck driver like his father and brothers.

Figure 14: Janetta with her son Harry and his wife Dorothy.

He married Dorothy Chesney on June 25, 1954 in Windsor, because that's where her father was working. They were both admitted into the Hamilton Sanitorium on June 30, 1954. Dorothy had tuberculosis on a lung; Harry had pleurisy. In March of 1955, Harry had a segment of one lung, the plural wall, and seven ribs removed. His recovery was very good with no disfiguration. Dorothy was discharged in June, the following year; Harry was discharged six months later in December of 1955. Their first son Harry Stanley Fanson was born on February 25, 1955 in the Hamilton Sanatorium. He was named after his father and grandfather, but he is usually called Butch. He was born exactly three years after his Uncle Bob died.

While Harry and Dorothy were in the Sanitorium, his brother Gord and his family rented Jacob's house in Fulton so they could be closer to Janetta's house and take her to the hospital to visit her son Harry and his wife Dorothy.

Harry William and Dorothy Fanson had four more children: Donald (Don), William (Bill), John, and Katherine (Kathy).

Brother Gord explained "I was driving my truck on Highway 3 and coming back from delivering a load to St. Thomas, when I passed my brother Harry driving to St. Thomas." After I passed him, I wished I had flagged him down to see if he wanted to stop for a coffee. Often, I would see one of my brothers on the highway and have a coffee with them. Later that night, I received a telephone call. Harry died in a truck accident."

Harry William was just 30 years old when a car collided with his transport truck on Highway 3, sending them both rolling over the embankment. He was taken to the St. Thomas Hospital on April 29, 1963, but he didn't make it. He had five children under the age of eight. They were destined to grow up without a father just like their father, and his father.

The Fulton United Stone Church still has service every Sunday morning. There is a cemetery and a hall for social activities. Author Barbara Fanson and some of her sisters were christened there.

The Fulton School was converted into a house in the 1950s. The current students of Fulton are bused to a school in Smithville.

Sam Madgers' General Dry Goods Store in Smithville operated until his retirement in the 1980s. Author Barbara Fanson used to get shoes and clothes at the store. Sammy Madger would always tell her stories of how he tried shoes on her dad when he was her age.

Thomas Merritt currently operates Merritt's Funeral Home in Smithville, which was established by his grandfather.

The Tweedside Wesleyan Methodist Church, which Janetta's uncles helped build, was demolished in 2004 by the city of Hamilton, because it hadn't been used for twenty years, and the building needed a lot of renovations. Janetta had heard the stories a million times of how her Grandfather John Tweedle and her uncles hauled all the bricks up the mountain by horse and wagon from the old Methodist Church in Bartonville to this new location in Tweedside. Bartonville is below the mountain on King Street near Parkdale Avenue. On Sundays, the Tweedside church was full of families with the last name of Tweedle, Althouse, Hildreth, and Springstead. (The church was opened in 1898 by its pastor, the Reverend Edward Whitworth. In 1925, the church became part of the United Church.)

Figure 15: Gordon, Harry, Robert, and Orval Fanson stand in their front yard with the Fulton Store and gas pump in the background.

Figure 16: Janetta's house in Fulton. Photo taken in 2001.

Figure 17: The Fulton Store has changed over the years.
This photo taken in 2001.

About the Author

This historical fiction novel is based on real people and real-life struggles. Author Barbara Fanson heard many stories and rumors of how her grandfather Harry Fanson died when her dad was only three-and-a-half years old. She also heard of the struggles her grandmother Janetta Fanson experienced trying to raise four boys under the age four during the worst year of the depression.

Barbara Fanson is a graphic designer, author, and retired college professor. This story is based on her grandmother and father.

Barbara grew up in Smithville, about 12 kilometers (7.5 miles) from where her Grandfather was killed in a car accident—and where her father was born. She lives near Hamilton with her husband, daughter, and a dashing black cat.

Other books by Barbara Fanson:

Producing a First-Class Newsletter, published by Self-Counsel Press.

Start & Run a Desktop Publishing Business, published by Self-Counsel Press.

From Desktop to Book Shop: Get your writing off the computer and into a book, published by Sterling Education Centre.

Headlines for Promotions: A helpful guide for planning advertisements, email marketing, and social media, published by Sterling Education Centre.

Visit our blog for tips on writing, designing, marketing, or self-publishing your own book:

http://fanson.net

Made in the USA
Middletown, DE
13 December 2016